The Heroic Life
of Al Capsella

J. Clarke

THE HEROIC LIFE
OF AL CAPSELLA

Henry Holt and Company ▪ New York

First published in the United States in 1990 by
Henry Holt and Company, Inc.,
115 West 18th Street, New York, New York 10011.
Published in Canada by Fitzhenry & Whiteside Limited,
195 Allstate Parkway, Markham, Ontario L3R 4T8.
Originally published in Australia by
the University of Queensland Press.

Library of Congress Cataloging-in-Publication Data
Clarke, Judith.
The heroic life of Al Capsella / by J. Clarke. — 1st American ed.
Summary: Fourteen-year-old Al Capsella, desperately trying to be
normal and blend in with the rest of the crowd, is constantly
embarrassed by his highly unconventional parents.
ISBN 0-8050-1310-5
[1. Parent and child—Fiction.   2. Individuality—Fiction.
3. Australia—Fiction.   4. Humorous stories.]   I. Title.
PZ7.C55365He   1990
[Fic]—dc20   89-24629

Henry Holt books are available at special discounts
for bulk purchases for sales promotions, premiums,
fund-raising, or educational use. Special editions
or book excerpts can also be created to specification.

For details contact:

Special Sales Director
Henry Holt and Company, Inc.
115 West 18th Street
New York, New York 10011

First American Edition
Designed by Victoria Hartman
Printed in the United States of America
1   3   5   7   9   10   8   6   4   2

For Yask and Angus

The Heroic Life
of Al Capsella

LAST NIGHT at 2:00 A.M. the phone rang. I heard my parents, the Capsellas, hurrying down the hall—there were soft little bumping sounds as they jostled each other to be first. I knew they thought something exciting was going to happen to them at last, and I even felt a bit sorry for Mrs. Capsella when she slouched into my room, all disappointed, and muttered, "It's for you."

"Who is it?" I asked.

"You don't have to worry," she replied rather snidely. "It isn't a *girl*. It's just Louis."

Louis is one of my oldest friends; we met ten years ago at Mrs. Dirago's kindergarten, or Never-Never Land, as the placed was called.

I picked up the phone. A familiar wheezing drone— Louis's asthma—came over the wire, so I knew something had upset him. "What's up?" I asked, kicking the door shut so the Capsellas wouldn't be tempted to eavesdrop.

He'd had a bad dream, the awful kind that starts off all smooth and nice and then, when you least expect it, starts going bad. He'd been on vacation somewhere up the coast, it was a great place, and he was having a great time. . . .

"I was having a great time—get that?" he repeated hoarsely.

"So? What's wrong with that?"

"Well—"

"Go on," I urged.

"I was a homicidal maniac!"

"Jeez!" I gasped, overdoing the astonishment a bit because I was smiling to myself. There's no way you could picture Louis as an ax murderer—he's too short. It's not his fault really; his parents are on the dwarfish side.

"I'd bumped off masses of people," he was going on, "fifteen or sixteen. I couldn't remember how, or what I'd done with all the bodies—all I could remember was the kidneys."

"The what?"

"The kidneys. I'd cut them out, you see—wrapped them up in plastic and buried them out back in Mom's fern garden."

"Not a very safe place," I remarked. Mrs. Cadigorn was always messing about in the ferns on weekends.

Louis ignored this. "You know what was the worst thing?" he cried, his voice going all high and funny. "I didn't give a shit! I knew I'd massacred all these people, but I didn't feel guilty or anything—it was just something I'd done, something ordinary, like putting out the garbage cans on Sunday night." He lowered his voice. "That's not normal, is it?"

I hummed a little tune under my breath. It certainly wasn't normal, but I didn't want to tell him that. Louis was a worrier.

"It was only a dream," I said casually.

"But that's the whole point! Don't you think having a dream like that might be a kind of sign?"

"Of what?"

"That—that something's surfacing! That I might be going a bit mad, becoming a psychopath or something?"

I considered the matter. Though I couldn't quite see Louis as an axman, I could easily imagine him as a psycho of sorts—you didn't have to be tall to be wacko in the head. Naturally I didn't say so; instead I thought back to all those late movies I'd seen where the shrinks interview loonies in gloomy padded offices. Those shrinks were always very busy with dreams, interpreting them and searching out symbols, rather like some of the teachers we had for English at school. Mrs. Slewt, for instance: She thought the baseball mitt in *Catcher in the Rye* was a symbol of compassion, and if anyone disagreed with her, she got really ratshit and shouted, "Don't be rude!"

"It's just symbols," I reassured Louis. "You know, the kind of thing Mrs. Slewt goes on about. The dream isn't really about murder or being a psychopath."

"What's it about, then?"

"Well—something you've been hiding and don't want anyone to find out. But something *you* don't really care about all that much."

There was a silence on the end of the line.

"Nothing very important," I prompted. "Something quite small and ordinary." The peculiar image of the kidneys in plastic wrap flitted across my mind—it must mean something. And all at once I had it! "The bio worksheets!"

I shouted. Louis hadn't handed in a worksheet all term; he was seven behind, and Parent-Teacher Night was coming up pretty soon.

"Those kidneys in plastic," I explained, "they're symbols, just like the burying's a symbol. And you don't feel guilty in the dream because it's not murder at all, just overdue homework, nothing really important. So you see, you're not a psychopath—you're perfectly normal."

"Yeah," agreed Louis. He didn't sound too happy about it. I suppose he didn't like being reminded about the bio worksheets—perhaps he'd rather have been a psychopath after all; it was less boring than homework, anyway.

"Take a day off," I advised him. "Tell your mom you've got asthma, stay home, and finish them all off. You'll feel better."

"Thanks," he said glumly.

Back in bed, I couldn't get to sleep. The phone call had started me thinking about being normal. When I was a little kid, I never thought about myself or other people this way, worrying about whether they were normal, or strange, or anything at all except themselves. People were simply there. It seems to me sometimes that I was happier when I thought in this simple way. Since I've gone on to high school, being normal has become a matter of importance: All of us are secretly worried that we might not be normal, that there might be something a bit odd about us, something that *shows*, that other kids can point to and laugh about.

Like my real name, for instance. It's . . . I can hardly bear to write it down . . . Almeric. The Capsellas, who are a bookish couple, found the name in *Coles Funny Pic-*

ture Book. It means "Work Ruler," as Mr. Capsella told me in his teacherly fashion when I complained about not being called Brett or Scott or Simon or even plain James.

"You'll be grateful when you're forty," Mrs. Capsella chimed in.

"Why?"

"Names like Brett and Scott were fashionable when you were born—they're all seventies names."

"Of course they are. That's why I wanted one—they're modern, not like Almeric."

"But don't you *see*? When you're forty and you've got a name like Brett, everyone will know your age. It's like flared jeans or those skinny shirts with pointed collars—people know how old they are. Almeric is ageless."

"Thanks a lot," I muttered. Not that it matters; no one at high school knows my real name. It's been "Al" so long that it's been forgotten.

All of us kids try hard to pass for normal, wearing the same clothes and hairstyles and being pretty careful about what we say and do in front of each other. But it's a difficult business: You're never quite sure you're being normal because you're never quite sure what being normal means. You can only be sure what's wrong, never what's right. And you always feel, somehow, that what you have is bound to be less normal than what others have. Sometimes I think it's a question of numbers, or being first. If you have a sweatshirt without a designer label it can be pretty shaming, but if three or four kids have the same shirt then it's not so bad—it might even become a fashion. At the moment it's abnormal to have a girlfriend, because no one in the freshman class has one except for Broadside Williams, and he doesn't count. But if four or five kids had girlfriends, then it would be all right, it would be normal, and not having one would seem strange. It's confusing.

Having normal parents is part of it. No one wants *visible* parents—unless they are pop stars or football players. Parents should be perfectly ordinary and unobtrusive, quiet and orderly, well dressed and polite, hardworking, and as wealthy as possible. Like children in the olden days, they should be seen and not heard. And preferably not seen very much at all.

The Capsellas are a real liability. Not Mr. Capsella—he's so vague and quiet, no one notices him much—but Mrs. Capsella does the one thing a parent should never do: She stands out. She's like an alien who's dropped in from another planet and doesn't know the customs—and she doesn't even try to learn. No, my parents aren't normal: Sometimes I think I should set them straight.

Take yesterday at school, for instance. Second period, room twenty-one; our class sitting watching Mr. Tweedie teaching Algebra. It was quiet and peaceful, and I was thinking over a problem I have, a fear of small monotonous noises like taps dripping or clocks ticking, when Broadside Williams nudged me sharply in the ribs. "Your mum," he hissed, jerking a meaty thumb in the direction of the window. I looked (so did everyone else) and there was Mrs. Capsella, horribly clad in jeans and a leather jacket, long scarf trailing out behind, weaving across the school yard on her bicycle.

The shame of it! My heart banged up against my ribs like it really shouldn't do in a kid my age. I'd warned her time and time again about coming to the school to complain about things: the books assigned for English, compulsory school uniforms, unhealthy food in the cafeteria, teachers hiding in the bushes to spy on girls who talk to boys behind the shower block—anything that took her fancy, really. I'd warned her off, but I'd known in my heart that the warning wouldn't be heeded, not for long, anyway. It isn't that she's a complaining sort of person: No, Mrs. Capsella is simply bored. At eleven or so in the morning she gets fed up with her lousy job—she writes those sloppy romances you see in railway newsstands—and then she casts about for something else to do. Mostly she rings up her friend Dasher and they'll go on a tour around the thrift shops, but if Dasher isn't available, then the school is very handy, just three streets away.

It looked like Dasher was out on this particular morning. Trapped in my seat, I watched while Mrs. Capsella skidded to a halt beside the railings and then tried to prop her bike up against them. It was a difficult business: The railings are thin and widely spaced, and the vehicle just kept falling through. Finally she chucked it in the azalea bushes and made her way up the steps. Even Mr. Tweedie was watching her now, and everyone in the classroom knew exactly what would happen next. Although she comes to the school quite often, Mrs. Capsella can never find the right door—she's like the really dumb rat you get if you come in late to the biology lab, "Bright Bertie," a cretinous rodent who can never find his way through the tunnels or flip the door with his nose like other rats.

She shouldn't have gone up the stairs at all, because the small door at the top is always locked. Visitors are supposed to cross the courtyard and go in through the main entrance, which is clearly marked. But Mrs. Capsella rattled at the handle of the small, unused door, and when it failed to open, she didn't turn and go away, but kept right on fiddling and rattling, exactly like Bright Bertie. After a few minutes Mr. Tweedie, a man much given to nervous tension, opened the window and stuck out his head. "I'm afraid you'll find that door locked, Mrs. Capsella," he called politely. The politeness didn't disguise the fact that he had her number; he knew that though she'd been standing there for several minutes rattling the knob, she still hadn't caught on that the door was locked.

When she heard his voice, Mrs. Capsella spun around, goggling upward. "Locked?" she called to the sky, and when no one answered, she lowered her eyes a little and spied Mr. Tweedie leaning out of the window. She came prancing down the steps, scarf flying, terribly pleased to see him. She's always like that after she's spent a few hours at her desk. Writing is not a profession I'd recommend to any daughter of mine. "Hullo!" she cried. "What are you doing there?"

What a question! A bunch of kids in the back row started giggling, and I didn't blame them. No normal mother would ask a teacher this kind of thing. And the question affected Mr. Tweedie oddly; he spluttered and turned brick red.

"Um—nothing," he replied. "That is, um, I'm teaching a class."

"Well, of course you are," agreed Mrs. Capsella, standing on tiptoe and peering into the room. She saw me and gave a little wave of her hand, and everyone waved back. A couple of kids said "Hullo," and Broadside Williams told her he liked her scarf and wanted to know if she'd knitted it herself.

Mrs. Capsella frowned. She said knitting turned you into a moron—hadn't he seen those ladies bumbling around the wool shop like poor old sheep who'd lost their fleeces and didn't know where to find them? She told him she'd bought her scarf at the thrift shop in Blaxland Place, and added, "You should go there, Broadside, it's very interesting."

Broadside Williams leered.

While this conversation was taking place, Mr. Tweedie stood by the window, wringing his hands. You could tell that he wanted to shut Mrs. Capsella up, but he wasn't allowed to be rude to parents. Besides, he was a small man with a soft voice, so he just went on wringing his hands, hoping she'd go away. There was no particular reason why she should; she had plenty of time on her hands. Then he took a deep breath—this meant he was preparing to speak a little more loudly than usual. "The entrance is over there, Mrs. Capsella," he said.

"Entrance?" echoed my mother in a vague, doltish tone. If Bright Bertie could speak, I know he'd sound just like Mrs. Capsella.

"The main door—it's to your right. You are going to the Mothers' Handicrafts Exhibition, I gather?"

"I didn't know there was one," answered Mrs. Capsella. "But if there is, I'll go." She put her head on one side. "I've often wondered about Handicraft Exhibitions."

She set off at a trot, scarf still flying. Other mothers walk: I'd noticed a few earlier in the morning, elegantly dressed, passing unobtrusively through the main entrance. They didn't have scarves and they didn't have bicycles; they came in Jettas and Hondas, parking them neatly in the visitors' parking lot.

Now Mrs. Capsella was fumbling with the catch of the main door, and we all held our breath. She was pulling the door out—it was the kind that opened inward. She performed this simple act for a full minute and a half, until Mr. Tweedie's nerve broke. *"In! In!"* he screamed.

Mrs. Capsella got in. She burst through, and the door closed smartly behind her. A sigh of relief broke from our lips, and Mr. Tweedie pulled his head back through the window. Our relief was premature; my mother's long woollen scarf was caught in the door.

"Can you beat that!" yelled Broadside Williams, wagging his big head about, and everyone grinned, imagining Mrs. Capsella bounding up the corridor and then being wrenched back, as if she were on elastic. We waited, expecting the door to open and the lady to emerge, sprightly and unabashed, to retrieve her dreadful scarf. But nothing happened at all: The door stayed firmly shut with the scarf dangling limply out of it.

An uneasiness began to settle over the classroom. Nobody spoke. Mr. Tweedie stayed by the window, tapping his fingers on the sill, a little frown upon his face. I was filled with irritation, and then, as we continued to wait and the door stayed closed and still, with a certain apprehension. A terrible thought crossed my mind: She might have *hanged* herself. It was ludicrous, impossible, it couldn't happen to anyone. And yet—it was just the kind of thing that might happen to Mrs. Capsella: a ridiculous death in a public place, completely abnormal.

I think the same idea occurred to Mr. Tweedie, for he

turned from the window and spoke to me. His voice was quick and nervous, as if he was afraid of making a fool of himself. He often spoke like this. "Er, Al," he said. "I think you'd better slip across and see how your mother's getting on."

No one laughed, which worried me even more. As I hurried across the courtyard, I reflected that instead of an epitaph in the bereavements column of the newspaper, Mrs. Capsella would appear on the front page, and in that tiny little paragraph titled "Odd Spot." I ground my teeth. How could any kid hope to pass for normal with a parent like that? I pushed at the door gently, fearing to find a dead weight against the base, but it opened smoothly enough and the scarf fell with a soft plop at my feet. There wasn't a sign of Mrs. Capsella, but away down the corridor I could hear the hum and cheep of ladies' voices, and my mother's, rising clear above them all, familiarly crying, "But do you *really* think so?" I gritted my teeth again, and finished the sentence in a savage and passable imitation: "It's very interesting—I've often wondered about that."

"Talking to yourself, Al?" called Mossy Crocket, the history teacher. I hadn't noticed her; she was lurking outside the staff room, enjoying a quiet, deathly smoke away from her healthier colleagues and cocking an ear to the chatter down the hall.

"Just practicing for something," I replied.

Mossy nodded her head. A gray cylinder of ash fell from the cigarette onto her batik blouse and burned a neat round hole. She didn't seem to notice; she yawned and hummed a snatch of song to herself. I recognized the tune: "Now Is the Month of Maying"—we'd learned it in seventh grade. Mossy smiled through her humming, tapping her foot in its homemade leather-work shoe in time to the song. She didn't ask me what I was doing roaming about the school during class time—like Mrs. Capsella, she always seemed pleased to see people.

I considered her curious garb: the batik blouse and lumpy, drawstring skirt, the red openwork stockings above the homespun shoes. By any normal standards she looked a sight, and yet after a while, after you'd got used to her, you didn't think that, you simply thought of her as Mossy Crocket—just as, I suppose, if Mrs. Capsella hadn't been my mother, I might just have thought of her as herself, as I used to do when I was a kid. And like Mrs. Capsella, Mossy always seemed pleased with her weird costumes—you could imagine her humming around her bedroom every morning, choosing oddities to wear, busy and happy and smiling to herself, while the Crocket family, if there was one, looked on in dismay. People like Mossy and Mrs. Capsella didn't seem to notice what other people thought; secretly I rather envied them this fine carelessness. But then they weren't fourteen, they didn't have to worry like I did, like Louis did, like all my friends.

I made my way back to room twenty-one.

"Everything all right, then?" asked Mr. Tweedie.

I nodded silently.

"I hope your mother enjoys the Handicrafts Exhibition," he said. "The mums have produced a very fine array of knitting."

Broadside Williams bleated like a sheep.

"That will be enough, Gerald," murmured Mr. Tweedie. He reached into his pocket and drew out a small plastic cylinder. Unscrewing the cap, he popped two small tablets into his mouth. It wasn't drugs—we'd checked up one hot day when he'd left his jacket hanging on the chair. It was an herbal remedy described as an "Executive Stress Soother." The brand name was Heroic Life.

2 THIS MORNING I had words with Mrs. Capsella about the matter of the socks. Morning isn't a good time to speak to Mrs. Capsella, because she often stays up till three or four in the morning, scratching away in her red-and-yellow exercise books. She sleeps late, so Mr. Capsella and I don't get proper cooked breakfasts like other families: Instead we find bowls of granola and glasses of orange juice set out neatly on the kitchen table. When I see those bowls there, so cool and tidy, I can never rid myself of the idea that Mr. Capsella and I are no more than domestic pets.

I knew it wasn't a good idea to wake Mrs. Capsella at a normal hour, but the situation had become desperate: For the last two weeks I had been wearing odd socks—not just varying shades of blue or gray, but different colors altogether: red and blue, and lemon and navy, and yesterday a mustard-brown check of Mr. Capsella's and a pale green number that I don't think even belonged to our family. People had begun to call me "rainbow feet." I stood at the bedroom door and called her name discreetly.

Mr. Capsella, emerging red and steaming from the shower, shook his head, warning me off.

"I have to," I said. "It's urgent."

"Well, do it quietly," he replied, sliding off down the hall.

"Mum," I called again, "I haven't any socks." I knew she'd hear; it's the kind of remark, however softly spoken, that would rouse her in her coffin, for she has an uncanny alertness to any whisper of what our Human Relations teacher calls "Home Duties."

At first she tried to get out of it. "Look in the back room," she mumbled, and settled down again beneath the eiderdown.

"I've looked," I said. "There's only odd ones."

"Well, *wear* odd ones then. You're not going to a ball, Cinderella."

I moved a little closer to the bed. "They're *too* odd," I said.

"Wear a pair of your father's."

"He hasn't got any either. He's been wearing sandals all week." Hoping to rouse a pang of guilt, I added: "It's winter, too."

Mrs. Capsella leaped out of bed. It's a queer thing, but when she gets up after three hours' sleep, she's never drowsy like other people; on the contrary, she seems more wide awake than usual; she moves faster, and her voice is more ringing than ever.

She rushed down the hall in the black thrift-shop mini-dress she wears as a nightgown, peering through open doors into odd corners of rooms, picking up bits of clothing as she went. "It's your fault," she muttered nastily. Mr. Capsella, who was standing beside a wire storage unit, sifting through its drawers in a quiet, methodical, scholarly fashion, blinked his eyes and winced slightly. Mrs. Capsella ignored him; it was me she was after. "You come in the house," she went on, "and take your things off wherever you like—if you put your socks in the laundry basket, this kind of thing wouldn't happen."

"We haven't got a laundry basket."

"Well, put them in the washing machine, then." She turned her back on me and began walking up the hall, making for the bedroom again. It was too much for me: I was sick of walking across the playground with sneering kids pointing at my feet. I was sick of the whole atmosphere at school: everyone so anxious to get at someone who wasn't quite right, as if by doing that, they'd be, somehow, mysteriously, righter. I turned on Mrs. Capsella.

"It's you," I yelled. "You lose them!"

Mrs. Capsella spun around. She drew in her breath slowly, like Mr. Tweedie when he wanted to make himself heard. With Mrs. Capsella it meant that she was endeavoring to control her temper; when she spoke, her voice was lower than usual, and all the words were separate, as if she were teaching a grade-one reading lesson.

"Look," she said. "I go through the house; I pick up all the socks I can find and wash them. If I can only find odd ones, that's not my fault."

"You hang them on the patio rail and forget about them, and they blow away." Here was another thing: Those windy days, walking home from school, glimpsing some familiar garment caught on a hedge or even hung up on a fence post by some thoughtful passerby. Kids hooking the thing off and kicking it along the street, yelling, "Look, some dickhead's lost his underwear!" Lucky for me she was

too lazy to sew on name tags. "You leave our cl[
over the suburb," I cried.

"I do not," said Mrs. Capsella swiftly, lying like a kid.

"Why do you hang things on the patio rail? Why don't we have a clothes tree like other people?"

"Because I won't have one of those ugly big things crowding up the yard, that's why."

"But—"

"Just be quiet for a minute, will you—let me think. There's a gray pair somewhere; I saw them yesterday." She darted into the living room, brushing past Mr. Capsella, who was eating his granola at the kitchen table in an anxious, hurried kind of way. I followed her and searched about in all the corners. I couldn't see any socks, but there were lots of things scattered about that you wouldn't normally expect to find in a living room: cricket bats and tennis balls and screwdrivers and old coffee cups and piles of newspapers. I thought of the living rooms I'd seen in other peoples' houses: all polished wood and spotless carpet, the wall units with china ornaments on the shelves and little spaces in between—nothing flung down in those spaces, no spanners or coffee cups or worn-out mousetraps. It grieved me sometimes. I felt deprived.

"This place is a mess," I sighed. "You should clean it up." Even as I spoke, I realized I'd made a mistake in the pronoun. It should have been "we," or even "someone": "You" was definitely wrong, and Mrs. Capsella prickled all over when she heard it. I knew that if this scene had featured in one of the psychodramas Ms. Rock makes us act out in Human Relations, my part would have been that

chauvinist porker. It occurred to me that chauvinist pork-
ers may well have begun their brutish careers as harassed
kids with no socks to wear.

Mrs. Capsella was going on. "These are *your* things,"
she cried, sweeping an arm about to indicate the cricket
bat and tennis balls, the tools and newspapers. She added
righteously, "Not one single thing here belongs to me.
I don't even read the newspaper. If you want it neat—
normal—" she amended, with something vicious in her
tone, "then *you* tidy it up."

"I wasn't born to tidy things up," I answered. I felt con-
fused; something had gone badly wrong with the sentence;
it wasn't my own—it was the kind of thing you'd expect
Mrs. Capsella to say.

Mr. Capsella hurried past us, his briefcase under his arm,
heading for the safe haven of the University.

"Did you hear that?" she called after him. "Did you hear
what he said to me?" There was no reply from Mr. Capsella, only his rapid footfalls on the concrete drive. She
turned back to me. "What do you mean, you weren't born
to tidy things up?"

"Well—if you really cared about what the house looked
like, instead of just pretending, then when I was a baby,
you would have taught me to put my things away."

"What?" Mrs. Capsella's eyes grew very round and
bright. Her face turned red. I thought she might be going to have some kind of seizure—she was about the right
age for it. But instead she burst out laughing. "Put on
your socks, Cinderella," she gasped, holding out the cob-
webby pair she'd found beneath the stereo, "and get out
of here."

I tried: The socks were very small. They barely covered my ankles. They must have been lying there for years.

As Louis and I turned the corner of Wentworth Street, the long low shape of the school plainly visible behind its grim wire fence, there was a rustling sound behind us. Louis looked quickly over his shoulder. When he was little, his father once read him a story called *The Silent Intruder*, and he's never forgotten it. He always sleeps with a cricket bat under his bed. He told me this as a secret, on the evening I told him about my sleeping problem and how, when I've got it, I take the clock down from the living-room wall and wrap it in my duffle coat. Now I watched as he flicked his head back, checking on the rustle. Even in daylight I knew he didn't feel quite safe. But when he turned back to me, there was a little smile on his face. "It's your mum," he said.

Mrs. Capsella was still wearing her black mini-dress. She had something else on top of it: a kind of hippie coat with fringes, which came down to her ankles. I hadn't seen it before; she and Dasher must have been shopping. I glanced quickly downward to avoid seeing it and found myself looking at her feet, long and bare upon the sidewalk.

"Hullo, Mrs. Capsella," said Louis cheerfully, just as if she were a perfectly normal mother. "How are you?" Louis has nice manners; he's been well brought up.

"Fine," answered Mrs. Capsella, beaming up at him. She is small and we are taller. "What a nice haircut you've got. It makes you look like John Cassavetes. Where did you get it done?"

"The Peppercorn."

"That's the place with the windows painted black and the ferns hanging over the doorway, isn't it?" asked Mrs. Capsella. "I thought it was a restaurant. Dasher and I tried to have lunch there the other day—"

I interrupted. As I've said, Louis and I have known each other since Never-Never Land, so he's used to Mrs. Capsella. But there were a couple of junior girls on the other side of the road; they'd stopped dead, pretending to examine the leaves on Mrs. Fleet's feijoa bush, as if they were looking for fruit. (It was well past feijoa time.)

"What's the matter?" I asked quickly. "Why are you here?" I wondered for a moment if Mr. Capsella had suffered a car crash on the way to the University, though it seemed too early for such news to have filtered through.

"I'm sorry about the socks," she said.

Louis glanced down at my feet. He couldn't see a thing; the socks had disappeared inside the rims of my shoes. A tittering sound came from the other side of the road, and a shuffle; the girls were moving on. One of them called softly, "Rainbow man!"

"It doesn't matter," I mumbled.

Mrs. Capsella gazed at me tenderly. "Poor thing," she murmured. "I just wanted to tell you I'm going to K Mart this afternoon to buy lots of new ones." She smiled and began walking backward on her toes, humming a little. "Tomorrow you'll be able to wear a proper pair."

"Thanks," I muttered.

She pranced a little. "Like normal people," she added.

When I got home from school that afternoon, Mrs. Capsella was hanging around by the gate. She was wearing jeans and a check shirt and looked comparatively ordinary: Lots of mothers in our suburb wear jeans in the garden. But Mrs. Capsella hadn't been doing any gardening; she'd simply been lurking about among the oxalis, waiting for me as if I were five years old. She has a thing about kidnappers and child molesters: I call it her Bunny Lake Is Missing Complex. You would never see Mrs. Cadigorn or Mrs. Palm hanging about their gateposts, waiting for Louis or James to get home from school. They're always getting the dinner ready or ironing shirts, or amusing themselves in some healthy way; it would never occur to them to start thinking about kidnappers or child molesters.

And I'm *fourteen*. Mrs. Capsella doesn't seem to realize this; she's always buying size-eight sweaters and having to take them back to the shop. I'm too *old* to interest a child molester, and when I tell her this, she seems to agree. "You're right," she says, embarrassed. She stays away from the gate for a couple of days, and then I find her back there again, pretending to look in the mailbox, a guilty expression on her face, so that despite myself I feel mean. Just as I feel mean when I try to stop her from picking me up after parties. "I'll get a lift," I assure her.

"Other mothers are allowed to pick their kids up—why can't I?"

"It's different with you."

"How?"

I can't explain. I don't have the heart to tell her how strangely she does it, coming up the path of the party house with a terrified expression on her face, crying out the instant the door opens, "Is Al here?" instead of saying, "Hullo, I'm Ellen Capsella, Al's mother. How do you do?"

She stands there, white faced, even trembling, repeating, "Is Al here?" And when the mother answers yes, Mrs. Capsella seems surprised, and if I don't get there quickly enough and bundle her out, she's likely to tell another of her stories: how, when I was three years old, she came to my new nursery to pick me up and no one knew anything about me. "Just like Bunny Lake Is Missing," she says. It wasn't really like that: I hadn't been kidnapped, nor merely mislaid. Even at three years old I'd realized there was something wrong with the name I had. I'd passed myself off as John, and the nursery teacher didn't know who Mrs. Capsella was talking about. "I always expect him to vanish," she tells the party mother, who looks at her oddly.

But on this particular afternoon, hanging about the gatepost, she didn't seem guilty. There was an excited flush on her face; she came right out onto the footpath and seized my arm. "Wait till you see what I've done," she cried.

She'd tidied the house. Amazing, isn't it? Most ladies tidy their houses every day; to Mrs. Capsella it was an extraordinary event, and she was terribly pleased with herself. She swept me along on a tour of the house, and I must say it did look neat with everything tucked out of sight. Though it was hardly what you would call clean: She hadn't done a thing about the cobwebs on the ceiling. I don't think she knew they were there. For a writer, she's very unobservant. I knew that if I mentioned them to her she'd say "What?" in her best Bright Bertie tone. And then, "I haven't got a broom that long."

"Now that it's all tidy you can ask your friends over without a blush," she murmured, and added, "poor thing."

"Mmm," I said.

On the table in my room there was an enormous pile of furry gray socks, at least fifteen pairs.

"Aren't they wonderful," enthused Mrs. Capsella. "And so cheap—three pairs for two dollars."

"No wonder," I muttered.

She didn't hear. "I got all the same color," she went on, "so if one or two get lost, you won't have to wear odd ones."

I thanked her, and kicked my shoes off. Mrs. Capsella pounced at once. "Not *there*," she said in a harsh kind of voice I hadn't heard her use before. "They have to go *there*." She lifted the corner of the eiderdown and showed me a plastic milk crate beneath the bed, with all my shoes arranged neatly inside it. "Everything has to go in its *place*," she said, her eyes glowing strangely. "No more kicking things off everywhere. And tell your friends as well. Look what I found today!" She opened the door of the wardrobe and drew out a big cardboard box heaped up with sweatshirts and track-suit pants and shorts and T-shirts. "No wonder their houses are neat," she remarked smartly. "All their stuff is here."

I opened my schoolbag. "Not *there*," cried Mrs. Capsella again as I chucked a couple of books on the bed. She leaped forward and retrieved them from the eiderdown, twitching the corners straight and placing the books neatly in the center of the table.

"I was going to put them there later," I said nervously. I was beginning to think that house-tidying wasn't good for her. She looked glittery somehow. She picked up my schoolbag and stowed it into the wardrobe, closing the door neatly. Then she went and flopped down on the sofa in the

TV room. I was surprised by this; she hardly ever watches Astro Boy. I fetched my after-school sandwich from the kitchen table and sat down on one of the beanbags; it was damp, and smelled of Pine-O-Clean.

The room seemed strange without its usual foliage of old magazines and cricket pads and T-shirts, like a tree stripped bare for winter: It even seemed colder. The sun was shining outside, and a yellow square of it beamed through the window onto the carpet. Mrs. Capsella glanced at the square irritably, as if she felt it shouldn't be there. "That carpet needs shampooing," she muttered. It was such an unusual remark for her to make that I couldn't think of an answer; I didn't have the practice. I nibbled at my sandwich; a few crumbs fell onto the floor and I noticed her eyes turn restively toward them. I scooped them up hastily. "That's right," said Mrs. Capsella. "And make sure you take that plate out." I rose to my feet. "No, no, not now," she said. "Relax."

I wished I could. But the tidy room got on my nerves; the damp, glistening beanbags seemed menacing, as if they were waiting for something rather nasty to happen. Then the ad I hate came onto the television screen: A very pleasant-looking woman in a pink frilly blouse is standing in a Dream Kitchen, listening to music on the radio. The music stops, and a voice begins talking about off-peak electricity. The lady bends low over the radio, nodding her head from side to side. "I love that," she says. The voice drones on about switching to off-peak electricity, and the lady strokes the side of the radio, a dreamy, besotted expression on her face. "I switched," she cries, picking up the radio, hugging it to her chest, dancing it around the floor. Normally I switch this ad off—so do Louis and James; it spooks us—but Mrs. Capsella, who hadn't seen it before, was watching with a horrified expression. "Good God," she said faintly. I noticed her hand, hanging limply down from the sofa.

I swallowed, and found myself saying, "You shouldn't worry about keeping the house tidy."

"What?"

"Well—I don't think Louis's house is all that tidy, or James's. They're just tidy in the front. The back rooms are all messy like ours." I wasn't sure that this was entirely true; I just suspected it from the way all the doors along the halls were shut, and the way James and Louis always said "Wait here" when they went to get something from the back.

"Well, why on earth did you make such a fuss this morning?"

"Just because of the socks. Now that I've got some, it doesn't matter."

"Mmm," said Mrs. Capsella. She sounded as if she didn't quite believe me. All the same, she sat up looking brighter and reached down under the sofa, dragging out some bulky plastic bags.

"Guess what Dasher and I found at the thrift shop," she said. "Wait till you see."

I sighed.

3 I LIKE WAKING UP on Sunday mornings, stretching my head out from under the covers and hearing that special, gentle quiet and, beneath it, all the sounds that aren't there on other days: the voices of little kids playing and people out walking in the reserve, the bell from St. Matthews, a dog called Winston barking on the other side of the hill, and the lawn mowers humming from gardens and nature strips all over the neighborhood.

Not from our garden, though. When you walk down our street, you can see our garden from a long way off, like a dense green jungle, with the couch grass and oxalis growing lush against the wall and the grass in the nature strip so high, it looks like we're growing crops instead of having lawns and flowerbeds like everyone else. When the Sunday walkers pass by, they peer over the wall and shake their heads, and sometimes Mrs. Whipsnoad, the neighbor across the road, brings her Sunday guests out onto her terrace just to take a look at our place.

I've spoken about the matter to the Capsellas. This is what happens: Mr. Capsella seems to be amenable, he accompanies me outside, limping slightly, though there is nothing wrong with his legs, he stares sorrowfully across the garden and agrees that it's a complete mess. But he doesn't turn on his heel and make purposefully for the garden shed; he just goes on standing there silently, staring and sighing.

He's depressed because he thinks of our house not as a place you live in, but as an investment. He says gloomily, "Yes, Al, the garden *is* ruined; we'll never be able to dump the house on anyone." He behaves like the whole mess is an act of God, the kind of thing that happens to people like him in this world: quiet, teacherly folk who don't start wars or rip off the system or disturb the environment. He acts like there's nothing anyone can do about it. He may walk slowly around the yard, tapping at bushes and tree trunks with a pen he's taken from his pocket and saying things like, "Once you've got blackberries, you can never get rid of them," but this is the limit of his physical activity. He returns to the terrace and worries: He thinks about the couch grass breaking up the paved paths, and the roots of bushes undermining the foundations, and trees falling on the house in a storm.

Then Mrs. Capsella arrives on the scene. Darting an accusing glance in my direction, she begins to cheer him up; she tells him the trees won't fall because they're quite young and strong, and the roots of the bushes won't get under the bricks because she's "keeping an eye on them." She concludes cheerfully that there's nothing really wrong with the garden except that the grass is too long and there are a few weeds, little matters that could be put right in a few hours. "So there's nothing to worry about really." When she says this, Mr. Capsella's gloom lifts, he stops being anxious about his investment, and quite cheerfully they both go straight back into the house and start reading again.

Mr. and Mrs. Capsella are great readers. They read by day and night, on weekdays and weekends, and even on vacations. They read at meals and while watching television, on public transport and even in other peoples' houses at parties, sneaking books out of shelves and sitting down with them in corners. They read anything; not just books and newspapers and magazines, but junk mail and the information on granola boxes and spaghetti cans. There's nothing wrong with reading—occasionally I do it myself—but it does strike me that there's something excessive in the Capsella's reading. They're readaholics; they can't go to the beach or watch a cricket match unless they have books in their hands to help them along. On Sundays, in particular, they lurk in bed till late, and when they do get up, it's just to look for a more comfortable place to read. If possible they always read lying down.

So I knew that if anything in the way of gardening was to be done, I'd have to do it myself, and last Sunday, a beautiful, still, sunny day with mowers humming all along the block, I set to work on the blackberries along the back fence. I cut them back and dug up the roots and piled all the scratchy stuff in a great heap beside the incinerator. Then I began on the oxalis. After an hour or so I began to feel a little tired and somewhat irritated; my hands were covered with scratches and there was gritty gray dust on my eyelashes and under my fingernails. I could tell from the sounds I'd heard from the house a while back—the jangle of cups and spoons, the fridge door opening, water running—that the Capsellas had gotten up from bed, and I knew from the silence there now that they'd slunk off to read on their sofas. I didn't see why they should be allowed to get away with it: Their reading was compulsive, a kind of disease.

I decided not to approach Mr. Capsella; I wasn't in the mood for his gloomy investment talk. There was another, more practical reason too. He was a bit accident prone when you got him working around the house: He'd start fixing something and then cut himself or do his back in, and then Mrs. Capsella would have to take him to the hospital. Without a license it was the only chance she ever got to drive, and she rather appreciated a small emergency.

The door of Mrs. Capsella's study was closed. When I opened it, I found her walking around and around the carpet, talking to herself. This was a pity; it meant she was actually working, making up one of her *Women's Journal* stories. " 'Raymonda watched the shadows lengthen on the lawn,' " she was muttering to herself. She seemed quite pleased, even eager, to be interrupted. I've noticed this before; if she's fiddling about at her desk or staring through the window or lying on the sofa, she hates to be interrupted, but if she's really working, she's delighted to see someone.

"Hullo," she said. "Where have you been?"

"Nowhere," I replied, somewhat sharply. "I've been doing some gardening."

"Heavens!" exclaimed Mrs. Capsella wonderingly. Then she added coyly, "You're a good boy." It made me mad; I began to complain about the rotten time I'd been having digging out the blackberries. "You could help," I finished up. "All the neighbors are out in their gardens."

"Trust them," she said.

"It's good exercise," I prompted. "You probably need it; you could have a heart attack the way you lounge about the house all the time."

"I don't think so," said Mrs. Capsella distantly.

"Plenty of people your age have heart attacks."

Some time back, one of her old pals, a guy she'd known at college, had dropped dead at thirty-nine; Mrs. Capsella had read about it in the paper, cried a little, and begun feeding us vegetarian food. I judged now from her thoughtful expression that my remark had freshened the memory. "Poor old Sam," she murmured. But still she sat there.

"And you could get fat," I added.

This worried her; she wouldn't be able to get into all those thrift-shop models if she put on weight. She followed me out into the garden, and I set her to work on the oxalis. She sighed and grumbled to herself as she moved along the bed, and every two minutes or so she'd raise her head and glance toward the windows of the house, and I knew she was thinking it wasn't fair that she should be slaving out in the open air while Mr. Capsella took his ease indoors. After about ten minutes she called me over and pointed out a small patch, about two feet square, farther up the garden, where the weeds seemed shorter than usual. She told me she'd weeded that spot last month, she'd spent a whole half-hour on it, and look, the weeds were all back again. I knew she was expecting me to say, "Oh, well, it's not much use wasting you time out here if weeds grow back again; you may as well go inside." I said nothing of the kind; my hands were still stinging from the blackberries. And really, she astounded me; she had no idea at all, she didn't understand, that most women spend a couple of hours a day in the garden. When I kept silent, she shuffled her feet a bit and then said, "I think I'll weed over there in the corner. It's easier to pull the stuff out when it's long; you don't have to bend down."

The oxalis was certainly thick in that corner next to the reserve. It reached halfway up the fence and was a very rich, deep green, as if it had been feeding on something. Mrs. Capsella pulled it out in great squishy handfuls and flung it down behind her, patches of rich black soil appeared along the fence. She seemed to feel she was getting somewhere at last. The sighs gave way to humming; I recognized the tune of Mossy Crocket's song "Now Is the Month of Maying" again. Then the humming stopped; in its place there was a queer, thick silence. I felt a rush of air at my back, as if a great bird was swooping down from the sky. I turned to find Mrs. Capsella standing right up close behind me, trembling all over and giving little squeaks under her breath.

"What's up?" I cried. I thought something might have bitten her: There were a lot of snakes about in summer, and though this was winter, I supposed she could have stumbled on a sleeping one.

"There's a *thing* in there!" she whispered hoarsely, grabbing at my sleeve.

"What kind of thing?"

She didn't answer.

"A snake?"

"No—no. A *thing*—" She put a hand up to her face. "Oh—it's awful!"

"But what kind of thing do you mean?"

"A thing—oh—it's an *eye*, staring up at me—a terrible great big open eye."

I looked down at my feet, slightly embarrassed. I'd been expecting something of this kind; that cheery humming had been a blind, designed to put me off the track. When her tale about weeds growing back again hadn't come off, she'd crouched down among the oxalis and busied herself thinking up another excuse to go inside. I'd been waiting for her to develop some kind of minor ailment, sore hands or a headache or dust beneath her contact lenses. I hadn't bargained on anything so crazy as an eye in the grass. It was the kind of dopey thing you'd find in one of her stories: some Laetitia or Madeleine finding a body at the bottom of the Squire's orchard.

"I'll have a look," I offered.

She followed me as I swished through the grass, tugging at my sleeve. "Don't!" she cried. "Don't go near it!" She skittered around to the front of me, barring my way, wringing her hands. "Don't touch it!" she repeated.

"Why not?"

She gulped, fishlike. "It's a baby."

"*What?*"

"I'm sure it's a baby—a baby's *head*. Someone's thrown it over from the reserve."

I stared thoughtfully at the clump of oxalis. It was true that the joggers and Sunday walkers were always chucking things over the fence, cans and bottles and bits of old iron; they wanted to keep the reserve tidy, and I suppose they thought we wouldn't notice a few more bits of rubbish on our lawn. But surely they'd never throw a baby over—they were healthy types, weren't they? All the same, I approached the place uneasily, and when I poked about with my spade I did it very cautiously. The weeds parted, something shone. There *was* an eye! An enormous, staring, glossy eye. It wasn't a baby's, though—it was too big and quite the wrong shade.

"It's yellow," I observed.

Mrs. Capsella gave a little scream.

"Babies don't have yellow eyes," I informed her reasonably. "So it's all right—you don't have to worry. It's probably just a dead lizard or something." I dropped the spade and took up a stick. Very gently I prodded at the head. The stuff around the eye was terrible, pus colored, and squelchy soft like an old wet towel. I squatted down to get a closer look, eye to eye. It *was* a towel, or rather, toweling material, very old and ratty. I turned it over. . . . It was a soft toy, a rabbit, the kind little kids take to bed with them. I fished it out and booted the thing across the grass toward Mrs. Capsella. She screamed and cowered against the gum tree.

"Don't *do* that!" she shrieked.

"It's only a toy rabbit," I said.

"It's a *baby*'s toy," she insisted. "I'm not going back near those weeds."

"What's going on?" Attracted by the screaming, Mr. Capsella had ventured out into the garden.

I explained the situation to him. "It's just an old toy someone chucked over the fence. Mum saw it in the weeds and thought it was a dead baby's head." Mr. Capsella smiled quietly to himself. Then he looked around the garden: He saw the weeded strips of the flowerbeds, the piles of blackberry and oxalis, and a curious expression came over his face. I knew it well: guilt.

"Hmm," he began. "Nice day."

Nobody said anything.

"I was just thinking of coming out to mow the lawn."

The hypocrisy of it! He'd never had such a thought in his life. He began to walk slowly down toward the garden shed.

"Oh—the mower," moaned Mrs. Capsella faintly.

I knew what she meant. Our mower could never be coaxed to start. I know other people have trouble getting their mowers started; you can hear them every Sunday pulling the string in and out and in and out, and swearing a little. But they only have to pull it out nine or ten times; last time Mr. Capsella pulled ours out thirty-seven times and still nothing happened, except that he went back inside the house, muttering to himself about bad investments.

"Don't *count*," Mrs. Capsella hissed in my direction.

But the warning wasn't necessary. It must have been our lucky day: six pulls and the mower roared into action, huffing clouds of black smoke all over Mr. Capsella's trousers. He trundled the thing out to the lawn and began mowing in strips, crunching over hidden tennis balls and bits and pieces of joggers' refuse. The mown strips appeared like tunnels with high green walls; the grass beneath was a deadly brown, and I could see that we were going to be odd men out as usual, the only people in the street with brown grass in the middle of winter.

Our garden lies on a slope, and Mr. Capsella soon got hot

and puffed, pushing the heavy mower up the hill and trying to stop it from rolling back on his feet. He started to turn red, and I thought of Mrs. Capsella's dead friend; Mr. Capsella was considerably older than thirty-nine. I took the mower from him. He gladly surrendered it and prepared to slide off unobtrusively into the house. Mrs. Capsella intervened: She suggested he might walk ahead of me and gather up the cans and tennis balls so we wouldn't break the mower and turn it into a bad investment.

As I churned along, I felt pleased with myself for getting the Capsellas moving: There they were, like normal people, working in the garden on a Sunday morning, getting exercise and fresh air and a sense of responsibility. But then, when I glanced over at Mrs. Capsella digging away at the paspalum beside the gate, and Mr. Capsella bending and straightening with his tin cans and yogurt cartons, for all the world like one of those bobbing toy birds you see in joke-shop windows, I couldn't help feeling slightly sorry for them. They looked miserable and oppressed, like a detention class picking up papers from the school courtyard at lunchtime. As I watched, Mr. Capsella came up slowly with a piece of rusty iron piping in his hand; he aimed it toward the fence.

"Watch it—you might hit a jogger or someone," I called. My warning simply brought a smile to his lips; he raised his hand to let the iron fly. But then something weird happened; the piping wouldn't come cleanly out of his hand, it seemed to stick there for a moment, and when it finally parted company with Mr. Capsella, there was a howl of raw pain.

You'd hardly believe it: He'd managed to get a big dirty

splinter of rusty iron imbedded in his finger! It was a nasty piece of work: Mrs. Capsella, eager to get her unlicensed hands upon a steering wheel, at once put down her spade and said firmly that she'd have to drive him to the hospital. Before you could say "Spring Garden" they were off. I couldn't help noticing that they seemed somehow pleased; even Mr. Capsella, with a piece of iron in his finger and the prospect of a bloody session with the doctor, looked happier than he had behind the mower. They liked it at the hospital; there were chairs to sit on and lots of magazines to read.

As the car rambled off down the road, I turned and surveyed the garden; it wasn't looking bad at all. Mrs. Capsella had been right—all it really needed was the grass cut and the weeds pulled out.

4 TODAY WAS SATURDAY, so it rained. On Friday afternoon, just after lunch, the clouds began rolling over; by nighttime the rain was falling, and kept on falling—and it's nearly summertime, too, it's almost November. The weather has changed; I'm sure it wasn't like this when I was a little kid, and thinking this gives me a nervous, frightened feeling, as if when I've grown up it will be raining all the time. It makes you start wishing you were young again, really young, before high school and grade school and even Never-Never Land, that you were a baby sitting on a rug on the lawn, enjoying the sunshine.

"That's negative thinking," remarked Louis.

"But it *has* changed," said James. "He's right."

The three of us were at my place for a Saturday night sleep-in. We've done this since we were quite little kids, setting up our sleeping bags and Louis's old portable black-and-white TV in the front room, and getting in supplies of potato chips and chicken crackles and chocolate-covered licorice from the drugstore. We watch the football replays and all the old films right up to the National Anthem at four o'clock in the morning. But mostly we talk, and it's funny how in the night like this we talk about things we wouldn't mention during the daytime, where it might seem weird. In the night it doesn't seem to matter somehow; you can say anything you like and no one laughs or holds it against you in the morning.

James said he'd read somewhere that it was getting colder all over the world, another Ice Age was coming, the seas and the land would freeze over, and there wouldn't be anything to eat and everyone would starve. This depressed us for a bit, until Louis remembered something *he'd* read, the same kind of article, only there it had said that the temperature was rising and the ice caps would melt and the seas come up and everyone would drown.

"I couldn't sleep for a week," he said.

"It's better not to read those kind of things," said James. "Or to think of them," he added morosely.

James has a gloomy face. He didn't always have it; last year, when he was thirteen, he had a round, jolly face like the kids in the margarine advertisements. Now he's gotten thin, the bones stick out under his eyes, and his chin is sharp: Mothers who haven't seen him for a while honestly don't recognize him. He's grown five inches in the last two months, and he's only fourteen. He's just over five eleven, and though all of us want to be tall, we don't really want to be tall so soon. There are years more for James to grow; if he keeps on going at the same rate, he could be eight feet high—he wouldn't be able to get under the railway bridge without stooping. Being scared about something like this makes you act differently, and James has become as gloomy as his face. He's always complaining, not only about the things you read in newspapers, which worry us all, but small things most of us have come to take for granted, like the watered-down tomato sauce in the school cafeteria, or the gritty soap in the showers, or the scented hair oil Broadside Williams always wears. Last year at the end of school, Mossy Crocket handed out joke awards to everyone in the class, neatly printed certificates with gold borders and fancy lettering: They looked real. Louis got "Most Assiduous Worker," mine was "Quietest Pupil," and James had "World's Worst Whiner." This bothered him a lot: Now, whenever he complains about something, he starts the sentence with "Don't think I'm whining, but . . ." Mossy Crocket, who meant to make him laugh, has given him another complex.

Louis and I are scared of ending up too short. We eat and eat, and do stretching exercises and weight-lifting, but neither of us has grown at all since August, and we're both only five two.

"Plenty of time yet," says Mrs. Capsella, who's only four eleven, just half a head shorter than Mr. Capsella.

Being fourteen is scary. It's like being in a fairy tale; you never know what you'll find in the mirror when you wake up in the morning: not just pimples or a hole in your front teeth, but something different and strange, like your nose growing big or your eyes getting small, things that can't change back again, so you know you're going to look like that for the rest of your life.

The dismal sound of the rain slapping against the windows reminded James of the Mormons: He'd seen them this very afternoon, he said, walking down Lawson Road in the rain, wheeling their bicycles. These two Mormons have been around our neighborhood ever since we were little kids, even babies. No one answers the door to them anymore, but still they keep on walking, two blond-haired American men in black suits who call ladies "Ma'am." When we were little, they were young—or so Mrs. Capsella says, young men with white mutton-fat skins and spots. Now they are practically middle-aged, their blond hair is thinning away, and their mutton-fat skin has wrinkles in it, but they still have spots. They seem old, walking along the streets with their bicycles, talking to each other. When you see them, you begin wondering where they live: You imagine a small, bare apartment above a hardware store and the two of them opening cans of beans and those tiny little red frankfurters that come from America. You wonder if they ever have time off, and if so what they do in it.

These two Mormons, who simply struck me as poor fish, people to wonder about, really worried James. They had a kind of fascination for him. Once, when he was five or six, he'd followed them. He'd walked for miles, till the familiar streets became unfamiliar and he didn't know how to get home again. He'd stood bawling on the footpath, and the Mormons had turned around and spotted him and kindly taken him home. They left him on his front porch, and Mrs. Palm, peering through the window, seeing the black suits and the pale spotty faces, wouldn't open the door for James until they'd gone away.

James was worried by his fascination; he was afraid it meant something, that one day he'd lose his grip, rush out, and become a Mormon, and forever after be walking about the streets of a suburb like ours, in a black suit, wheeling a bicycle, with little kids feeling sorry for him. I suppose, secretly, he felt he might be that kind of person.

Louis seemed to sense this, for he said suddenly, "You're not like them."

"Really?" said James hopefully. "Then why do they bother me so much?"

"Because—" began Louis slowly.

"Yes?"

"Because . . . I know what it is!" He giggled.

"What?"

"When you were a baby, when you were *two weeks* old, they looked into your carriage in the shopping center. That's all. They kind of imprinted themselves on your mind."

"You could be right," I said. "They do look in baby carriages."

James was quite cheered up. His gloomy face lightened a little.

But there was Louis. From the corner of my eye I saw his hand steal up toward his chin, and I looked away quickly. Several times lately I've seen him walking along the street by himself, slapping the underside of his chin with the back of his hand in a brisk fashion. When he sees someone coming, he pretends to be scratching, just as people who talk to themselves pretend to be singing if you catch them. Well, at least that meant he knew he was doing it.

He was at it now—slap, slap, slap—quick, smooth little pats, like a lady putting on face cream. Although the television was on and the rain was roaring down the gutters through all the holes Mr. Capsella never got around to fixing, the slapping sounded quite loud because we'd stopped talking and it was the only human sound in the room. I glanced at James; he had his head down and was drawing a pattern on the carpet with his finger, very slowly and carefully. So he'd noticed too. I closed my eyes so I wouldn't have to watch. Then the slapping sound stopped, and Louis said in a strangled voice, "I've got a double chin."

So that was it! Now it seemed all right to look. But though we peered pretty closely, we couldn't see any double chin. Louis's face is rather round, like James's was before it went all sharp and narrow, but he's not really fat, and I thought his chin looked just the same as it always has.

"No, you haven't," I said.

"Yes, I have—look!" Louis pushed his chin down toward his chest. "See? Double chins!"

"But everyone has a double chin if they press their head down like that; it squishes the skin out." I pressed my chin down. "See, now I've got one too. It's just a phoney double chin."

"So have I," said James. But he hadn't really; even pressed down, his chin stayed sharp and pointed.

Louis wasn't so easily persuaded. First he said his double chin was fatter than mine and that this meant he'd really have one when he was older. He seemed unwilling to give up the idea, as if he'd grown attached to it, as if he'd been thinking about it for so long that it had become a real part of him, like a mole or a wart, and though it bothered him, he was sad to see it go for good, a little piece of himself sliding into nowhere.

"Don't think about it," advised James. "Thinking about things makes them happen. That's how you get white hair."

"Or get fat," I added. "Like Rosy Canute."

Rosy was a girl in our class who had once been normal size. She read a lot of those glossy girls' magazines that tell you what you should be wearing and looking like, and she began worrying that she was fat. Worrying made her want to eat; she ate cakes and Mars bars and whole economy-size tubs of ice cream. While she was eating, she didn't worry; her mind went blank the moment she opened the fridge door. Pretty soon she was fatter than she'd ever feared.

I thought a lot about this kind of problem: how worrying seemed to make things happen, how you could bring about what you most dreaded simply by concentrating on it. Such a thing had happened to me when I was in seventh grade: I fainted in morning assembly just because I'd begun to imagine how horrible it would be to faint, to sink down on the gritty asphalt in front of everyone, with people crowding around you to get a look, and then being carted off to the sickroom by the phys-ed teacher and a couple of brawny toughs from the senior class, with your head lolling and your legs and arms dangling down foolishly. As I thought about it more and more, my heart began thumping and I began feeling hot and dizzy, and then I fell down, exactly as I'd imagined it. Afterward Mrs. Capsella took me to the doctor, who peered into my eyes with his little light, searching for brain tumors. He didn't find any; he said that boys my age often fainted for no reason at all.

"But I *had* a reason," I told him. "I was *thinking* about it."

"Think of something else," he advised me shortly.

On the way home in the taxi, I had an argument with

Mrs. Capsella about heart attacks. It seemed to me that if you could faint just from thinking about it, then you might well manage to have a heart attack from the same cause. You might even be able to die that way. Mrs. Capsella said smugly that I was too young. She spoke as if heart attacks and sudden death were the prerogative of middle-age, like R-rated movies.

"Think *positive*," she said. She even bought me a cheap-looking booklet on Positive Thinking. It didn't help; it read like something a Mormon might have written.

But James must have read it, because now he said to Louis, "The best thing is to keep on thinking, all the time, that you're really good-looking and it's only the other people who have things wrong with them. Like Broadside Williams."

Broadside Williams is the ugliest kid in the school. Everything is the wrong size: his nose is too big, his eyes are too small, his ears stick out, and his chins wobble down the place where his neck should be. His legs and arms don't seem to match up, as if his mom bought all the bits in a thrift shop and tacked them together by candlelight. He's fat too, much fatter than Rosy Canute: 375 pounds and only five foot two. He wobbles and rolls about the place, but he doesn't seem to think he's ugly at all; he's always peering into mirrors and combing his hair and smirking to himself. And he doesn't *act* fat, not like the skinny worried girls who won't use the top cup on the watercooler because it might have a finger mark inside it, and finger marks are human grease and grease is fattening. Broadside eats what he likes: cupcakes, and jam doughnuts with cream, and malted milkshakes.

Last year, when he joined our phys-ed class, we all imagined Broadside would be a bit embarrassed, stripping off in the showers afterward and revealing his jelly rolls. Not a bit of it; he seemed proud of himself. He even began pointing at *us*; he'd point at our balls and double up with laughter, hugging himself around the middle and gasping and wheezing for breath. Something weird happened then. I still can't understand how it came about: None of us said a word to each other, yet all at once every single boy in the class except Broadside was wearing his underpants in the showers, something we'd never done before. Phys ed was first period, so we were wet and frozen all day long, and people began getting colds all the time.

Then Oswald Padkin got pneumonia and Mrs. Padkin came up to the school, complaining about poor boys being forced to wear their pants in the showers, as if the place was a kind of seminary. No one told on Broadside Williams, and the principal got the idea that we were doing it out of modesty or something. He gave us a lecture on Being Proud of Your Human Body and said he was surprised to see unhealthy prudery linger on in this day and age: It was the kind of thing that could give a school a bad name.

Broadside Williams clapped loudly and cried, "Catch me wearing underwear in the showers!" But he stopped pointing and giggling. He now had other things on his mind; he'd acquired a girlfriend, Sophie Disher, one of the skinny types who wouldn't use the paper cups from the watercooler. It's a mystery to me how she can bring herself to touch Broadside Williams; he's got a lot more grease on him than a paper cup.

While we were discussing Broadside, and how it was that the most depressing-looking person in the whole school acted like he didn't know what the word depression meant, there was a bit of noise and clatter in the driveway as the Capsellas arrived home. I lifted a corner of the curtain and saw them walking across the patio, Mrs. Capsella a little bit in front of Mr. Capsella and moving briskly, as if she was annoyed about something. In a moment I saw what she was cross about: Mr. Capsella had let The Shadow follow them home again.

The Shadow is a friend of Mr. Capsella's. His real name is Casper Cooley, and he was once married to Mrs. Capsella's friend Dasher. He is a man of about forty-five who is always following people home. When he was married to Dasher, he used to follow Mr. Capsella home from work and sit in our living room for a long time, talking about Life. Mostly he talked about how dull it was to be married and to live in the suburbs, how dispiriting it was to go home every evening to the same house and the same routine and the same people. Nothing exciting ever happened, he said, and yet you never got any peace either.

Sometimes he talked about his childhood, which seemed rather distressing. He was particularly bitter about the way his mother had left him locked up in a cupboard while she went out to have a good time at the Communist Youth League.

I never knew whether to believe this or not. It was always like that with The Shadow: You couldn't figure out, when he told you his sad stories, if they were true or not. It was the look on his face that made you suspicious—a strange, excited expression—and he talked very fast, too, as if he was afraid you were going to question him and he had no intention of giving you the chance to get one in. And if you did get a chance, even if you just said, "Really?" he'd change the story around a bit. When he first told me the one about his mother locking him up in the cupboard, I did say, "Really?" I spoke in amazement rather than disbelief, but straight away The Shadow said that it hadn't really been a cupboard, just a very small room that *felt* like a cupboard.

He had a thing about the "True Woman." A True Woman was a lady who stayed home and cooked meals and looked after the children and waited at the window for her husband to come home at night: If he didn't come, she just turned from the window with a gentle sigh and went on with her knitting. She never complained, because she really *liked* that kind of life. True Women did. They loved cooking and kiddies and keeping house; it was natural to them. When The Shadow talked in this vein, Mrs. Capsella ground her teeth and Mr. Capsella seemed embarrassed. I felt they were a little hard on him. You could see that he'd never done Human Relations at school, just as you could see he didn't really know much about girls. I couldn't imagine any of the girls in our class waiting for hours at windows and enjoying it. I mean, nobody really would, unless there was something a little bit wrong with them. The Shadow didn't know this; he was sad because neither his mother nor Dasher had been True Women. I suppose it was a bit like believing in Santa Claus and feeling that your life was spoiled because he didn't really come down your chimney on Christmas Eve.

When Dasher ran off, I thought The Shadow would go

out and have an exciting time, catching up on all the Life
he'd missed out on while he was married. But he didn't.
He still follows people, and I don't mean girls, either. He
follows the Capsellas and other married people, he follows
them home from parties and sits talking in their living
rooms, just as he always did. Only now, instead of complaining about married life and suburbia, he talks about
how lonely it is to be a single man, how sad it is to go back
to an empty apartment at night with no one waiting for
you, no dinner ready, and no one to talk to. Everyone else
has a home and a wife and kids, they hurry off to their
families after work, and he is left out. Locked out of the
cupboard, you might say, instead of being shut up inside.

5 "SHIT! Who's that old tramp with your parents?" cried James. He'd come to the window to get a look at the Capsellas wading through the rain.

"It's not a tramp; it's a university professor," I explained. "He's a friend of my parents. And he's not as old as you think; he's only about forty-five."

It was true that The Shadow did look considerably older than his years. He'd let his hair grow back into the style he'd worn when he was a student, an Afro of sorts. But his hair wasn't really curly enough for an Afro; instead of standing out from his head, it sank down about his neck in a hopeless, greasy kind of way, and when he wore his old brown raincoat he did look a bit like a park-bench case. He was proud of the raincoat; it was something called a Burberry, which his aunty had sent out from London; he'd shown me the label on the back of the collar. The Shadow was always showing people things: Once he showed me a rash on his leg and asked if I thought it could be skin cancer. I was taken aback; I didn't really know what skin cancer was supposed to look like. I peered at the piece of leg he was showing: The flesh was red and spotty and slightly inflamed. It looked like diaper rash to me.

"What do you think?" The Shadow asked me eagerly.

I replied that I didn't think people got skin cancer on the backs of their knees; it was generally on the face and hands, places where you get sunburned.

"I don't get much sun," said The Shadow gloomily. He'd rolled his trousers down again in a disappointed fashion. There was a story that once he'd asked a lady at a party to look down his throat with a flashlight.

Although I considered Mrs. Capsella was a bit hard on him—lately she'd taken to leaving the house when he followed Mr. Capsella home—The Shadow did bother me a bit. He liked to get you on your own and ask questions; they were always very private questions, ones you felt uneasy about answering. He often asked me if I had a girlfriend, and when I said no, he wanted to find out why not. I couldn't think of a reply; I didn't want to tell him how everyone in our class was waiting for someone else to be the first. I could see that he'd find this answer unsatisfactory; he probably wouldn't even believe it. I got the feeling he was waiting for me to say I was too ugly or that girls didn't like me; he seemed to want to hear sad news about everyone. He liked to call people "poor"—"poor old Rob," or "poor old Tom," and so on. I didn't want him calling me "poor old Al."

When I didn't answer his question about the girlfriend, he asked me if I was feeling depressed. "No, not at all," I replied, and he seemed to fade a bit, like a ghost who meets up with a strict nonbeliever.

"When I was your age, I was always depressed," he said, shaking his head so that all the limp locks waggled. "Gee— was I depressed! It's a real bad scene, being fourteen."

Now, I've often thought that myself, but when I'm with The Shadow I find myself saying quite the opposite; I act like I don't have a care in the world, or a nerve in my body—anything so he won't go around calling me "poor old Al."

Sometimes he asked me about the Capsellas. He wanted to know seedy things like how old they were and whether they slept in the same room or in separate ones, and what Mrs. Capsella did all day and whether she went out at night by herself. I always answered, "I don't know," so he probably thought I was a moron. I could imagine him going around to some other married people's house at night and asking, "Have you met the Capsellas' son, poor old Al? What do you think of him?" They'd probably say, "We don't know," and I could picture him shaking his head and telling them that I had a lot of problems.

Outside in the rain, the Capsellas were having problems getting the door open. While Mr. Capsella fiddled with the keys, Mrs. Capsella was doing her level best to get rid of The Shadow. I could hear her through the window, telling him he'd been very kind to see them home and now he'd better get home himself as it was very late and he'd got a little damp in the rain. She could have saved her breath.

"I'll just dry off inside," The Shadow replied; and quick as a flash he'd whipped the keys from Mr. Capsella's uncertain fingers and got clean inside.

I turned the lights out in our room; I didn't want them coming in. Out in the kitchen I heard someone opening the fridge and Mrs. Capsella's voice brightly exclaiming, "Oh, *no*. There's no milk for breakfast! I'll have to go to 7-Eleven."

Muttering sounds came from the living room. I knew this would be Mr. Capsella advising her against such a jaunt. He's nervous about Mrs. Capsella in just the way she is nervous about me: He thinks the parking lot at the 7-Eleven is full of thugs and muggers just waiting to get their hands on her. And he didn't like her driving the car without her license. Going to get groceries was hardly an emergency.

The door of our room opened quietly, and there stood Mrs. Capsella. She switched on the light and glanced quickly around the room, counting heads, checking up that no one had been lost or kidnapped while she was out. "Good, you're all here," she murmured happily.

Louis giggled and tried to turn it into a cough. Mrs. Capsella peered at him anxiously. "How's your asthma, Louis?" she inquired.

She shouldn't have said this. Louis hardly ever gets asthma now, unless someone reminds him. He remembered now; in an instant his breathing became louder, and he began fumbling beneath his sleeping bag, searching for his Primatene.

"I vacuumed all the carpets so the dust wouldn't bother you," Mrs. Capsella continued.

I said quickly, "Louis doesn't get asthma anymore."

"Don't you?" asked Mrs. Capsella doubtfully.

"Not really," said Louis. "Not badly, I mean." He pushed the Primatene back out of sight.

"That's great," said Mrs. Capsella. She stepped farther into the room, closing the door behind her. "Did you see who came in with us?" she whispered.

"The Shad— Casper Cooley."

"That's right, Casper." She frowned. "I'm absolutely fed up with him; he's been following us around all night. I'm going to bed and your father can listen to him. But I don't want him to know I've gone to bed."

"Because he'll be hurt?"

Mrs. Capsella smiled grimly. "Not exactly. I just don't want him coming in there and telling me how his mother used to put plastic pears in his school lunch-box."

"Because she wasn't a True Woman."

"That's right. So I want you to listen, and if you hear him going up the hall, just remind him I've gone to 7-Eleven to get some milk."

"But when he goes home, he'll see the car and know you haven't gone," said James. "And then he'll come back inside to see where you are." James catches on to things fast.

Mrs. Capsella shot him a grateful glance. It was the kind of small, important detail she'd never think of herself.

"You could go out and move the car," I suggested. "But you wouldn't be able to get back inside without him seeing you."

"That's okay," said Mrs. Capsella. "I'll come in through the back window."

So off she went, jingling her car keys ostentatiously, with Mr. Capsella calling out warnings about the muggers in the parking lot. We heard the car start off down the road, and a few minutes later faint rattling and scuffling noises in the back of the house as she climbed in through the window. Then everything was quiet again, except for the rain and the flickering of the TV set (we'd turned off the sound) and the dull whine of The Shadow's voice as he told Mr. Capsella about himself. When you couldn't make out the words, it was a soothing sound, a bit like the rain, and just as endless.

I woke up much later: It must have been about three o'clock, because the late late movie was still playing. Light from the kitchen shone into my eyes; someone was opening the door. It was The Shadow.

He had a funny way of coming through a door. He didn't open it and walk on through like most people do. First he pushed it a tiny way, with the tips of his fingers, making a space just big enough to slip his big head through, then he opened it a fraction more for his shoulders, and then the rest of him sidled slowly around the edge. The expression on his face always seemed to suggest he was thinking he wasn't welcome, that the people inside the room were going to throw him out. Because of this you felt guilty, so you let him stay; and then, somehow, you felt tricked.

The Shadow advanced across the room, ducking his head politely. He was wearing his Burberry. It was very long, almost down to his feet, as if his aunty had bought it many years back, at a time when The Shadow was still growing, and he'd never really gotten big enough for it. "Hi, guys," he said, wiggling his fingers at us.

Louis and James stirred into life down inside their sleeping bags, groaning a little. I switched on the light.

"Ouch," moaned James, putting his hand over his eyes. Louis turned his head in The Shadow's direction, grinning to himself. They'd met before—I think Louis rather liked him, but then, it was easy for him; he didn't live in our house and he could always get away.

"Where's Dad?" I asked.

"Your dad's gone to sleep on the sofa," replied The Shadow. There was a trace of resentment in his voice. He began prowling around the room, picking up things and turning them over in his fingers. He took my class photo down from the shelf and studied it closely. "Which one's Ellen?"

"Huh?"

"Which one's your mother?"

"That's my class photo; she's not in it." I added, "They don't put the mothers in."

He shook his head from side to side again. "It's the hair," he said vaguely.

"How do you mean?"

"It's this short back and sides you guys wear, like squares did back in the fifties—made me think it was an old photo."

"It's got this year's date on it."

He squinted closer. He has glasses, those hippie spectacles with gold rims. I suspected the prescription wasn't quite right; probably Dasher had bought them for a song in the thrift shop. "Hmm," he said, "I thought it was 1966."

"Mum wasn't even at school in 1966; she left years before that." My remark was careless. Mrs. Capsella was cagey about her age.

The Shadow was so pleased, his spectacles flashed like beacons. I had that tricked feeling again. "Where *is* your mother?" he asked. "It's ten past three and she hasn't got back from 7-Eleven." He smiled and lowered his voice. "I don't want to worry you, but do you think she could have had some kind of accident?"

"She has a friend at 7-Eleven," I lied. "They talk all night. That's why she goes there, really."

The spectacles glinted again; it was rather spooky. "What kind of friend?"

"Just a friend. Someone she knew at school."

"I thought she went to school in Sydney."

"She did. But people move around."

"Do they?" he asked sadly. I suppose he was thinking of Dasher; she certainly moved around.

"Is it a man or a woman?"

"What?"

"Your mother's friend."

"It's a woman."

The Shadow smiled.

I said, "I've met her; her name's Leonie."

"Leonie, eh? I might go across and look them up. Where is the 7-Eleven exactly?"

"Miles away. Leonie's really old—about fifty."

"I thought you said she went to school with your mother."

"She was a bit slow. And it was a big school, one of those that go from kindergarten to high school."

"She must be an interesting kind of person if your mother spends so much time with her. I think I'll—"

"She's a feminist," I said bluntly.

"Oh," said The Shadow weakly. Dasher was a feminist. He sank down on a beanbag and stared at the TV screen. Something caught his attention there.

"Hey," he said. "That's Elke Sommer. Shit, she looks old."

"She *is* old," said Louis, joining the conversation.

"No, she's not," said The Shadow aggressively. "She's younger than m— I mean, younger than your father."

"That's pretty old for a film star," said Louis mildly.

James groaned. He was rather slow at waking up; I don't think he liked it much. I suppose when he woke up, he began remembering that he was over five foot eleven and only fourteen years old. The Shadow reached out with his foot and prodded at the end of his sleeping bag. "Wakey, wakey," he said. James pulled the covers over his head.

"How old do you think I am?" asked The Shadow, turning his attention back to Louis and me.

It was a difficult question; I found myself blushing. It wasn't that I didn't know the answer; it just seemed rude to give it. "Um—thirty-nine," I said.

"Come off it," cried Louis. "He's fifty if he's a day."

The Shadow glared at him. "You're a hard little kid," he said. "Do you know that?"

"Well, forty-nine," said Louis. "I was only joking."

"Some joke," muttered The Shadow. "You'll go far with a sense of humor like that." He turned to me. "Watch this," he instructed. He grabbed the fleshy, saggy bits at the bottom of his cheeks and pulled them back toward his ears, tightly. "How do I look now?" he asked. "Do you think I look better like this?"

"How do you mean?"

"Well—younger?"

"Gee—um—suppose so."

"Don't have a facelift," said Louis seriously. "They do them with lasers now; it doesn't always work. You can come out with one side of your face up and the other side down, like you've had a stroke. I read it in *Time* magazine."

"Did you now?" said The Shadow menacingly. Then he

began talking about football. From what he said, you could tell that he'd never played a real game in his life; it was all poetic stuff about running across a field in the early morning and feeling *alive*, with the grass wet and crunchy under your feet and your lungs full of crisp, cold air. Then he got on to girls. I knew he was going to do this; it's as if all the other things he talks about are just a kind of pretence to show that he's a normal sort of person with other interests.

He asked us if we had any big girls in our school. I couldn't figure out what he meant, and even Louis seemed stumped. We didn't know if he meant older girls, like the ones in the junior and senior classes, or tall girls, or the ones Mrs. Capsella calls "well developed." There was quite a silence while we puzzled over this and The Shadow waited for our answer.

James was awake now; he sat up, rubbing his eyes, and asked sleepily, "Do you mean girls with big—er, good— figures?"

"Good figures, eh?" grinned The Shadow. He wagged his head about. "No, no—*actually*, that's not quite what I had in mind. I meant BIG—" He waved his hands about. "*Huge*, you know, like hulks."

"Fat girls?" asked James, puzzled. The fat girls in our form are short. They're little, really, except for the fat.

"Not fat, exactly," said The Shadow. "Just huge—girls like towers: tree-trunk legs, arms like Christmas hams, great big moon faces." He sank down in his beanbag, spreading his legs out. A knee clicked horribly. He lowered his voice and began on a story. "I was a small kid, you see; at fourteen I hadn't, well, developed."

Louis giggled. Like me, he thought "developed" was a word mothers used about busty girls.

"A little, weedy, white-faced kid," droned The Shadow. "I went to Box Hill High. There was a big girl in the junior class. She had a friend, not quite as big as her, but pretty hefty. They used to follow me about—they used to *wait* for me, in the afternoons after school, down by the cycle shed. They had *bikes*." He made the word sound like a weapon. "You had to go past the cycle shed to get out the gate; there wasn't any other way. I used to hide out in the boys' lavatory, waiting till they'd gone, though I never felt safe even there. They were the kind of girls who wouldn't think twice of going into a boys' room—even crawling about on the floor, looking under the doors. And this particular afternoon they were waiting for me, they ran out and tackled me, they brought me down, they dragged me into the cycle shed and the BIG one began kissing me. All I remember is she had this enormous, slobbery mouth—"

Louis began to wheeze.

"Do you think Collingwood will make the playoffs?" I asked him to take his mind off his asthma.

"They've a chance," he murmured politely. Louis was a Hawthorn fan; normally he'd have said "No way"—but The Shadow had the effect of making us gentle with each other.

Our small conversation seemed to hold no interest for him; it was as if he'd forgotten there was such a thing as football. "She had no *teeth*," he was saying.

James was fully awake now, and sharp as a tack. "No teeth at all?" he asked.

The Shadow heard. "Huh?" he muttered uneasily.

"I'm asking about the *teeth*," prompted James. "Do you mean she had false ones and took them out to kiss you?"

"No, no. She had *some* teeth, back ones. Just the front ones were missing."

"You mean she hadn't gotten them yet—like she was a big eight-year-old, a gifted child they'd put in high school?"

"What? No, no." The Shadow shook his head irritably. "She lost them."

"How?"

"I hate to think. Anyway, as I was saying"—his voice rose, drowning out James—"I got *away*, and ran down Birdwood Street into the park. I could hear them coming after me on their bikes, ringing their bells and screeching and cackling. I tripped and fell. Do you know, they ran straight over me! There was a tire tread printed on my shirt. I had to hide it in the trash so my mother wouldn't find it."

"Why?"

"Well—I didn't—"

"It must have hurt," said Louis soothingly. "Did they break a rib or anything?"

"No," said The Shadow. "There was no *physical* damage. No physical damage at all." He sighed.

James sank back down into his sleeping bag. You could see his lips forming the word "Bullshit."

I think we were all wondering if the story was true. I suppose it must have been, because there didn't seem to be any point in making it up. I mean, why would you?

"Do you boys ever go to Box Hill?"

"Why should we?" muttered James irritably. "There isn't anything there."

"I haven't been to Box Hill since I left school," The Shadow confided. "I'm too scared I'll see *her*, serving in a butcher's shop, slapping hunks of meat about on a slab."

"She wouldn't still be there," I said. "Not after thirty years."

"Twenty," said The Shadow quickly.

"Well, twenty—she'd have gone somewhere else."

"Not a girl like that," he answered. "Those kind of girls never move; they stay in the same place."

"Why?" asked James. "Why should they?"

"She might have become a nurse or something," said Louis. "She might have gone overseas."

"Not her," said The Shadow.

There was a long silence. The television flickered, the rain spattered on the windows. James crawled back into his sleeping bag, but I knew he wouldn't be allowed to sleep just yet. And I was right. The Shadow sighed and shook his head. "I suppose you guys know all about the facts of life," he ventured seedily.

"We learn it in school," I said. "It's called Human Relations."

"You don't know how lucky you are. My mother taught me the facts of life. She wasn't a True Woman, she never talked to me, she just gave me a book to read, a *Nurses' Almanac* she'd picked up somewhere. It was full of warnings about the evils of jerking off, how it stunted your growth, gave you brain damage. It frightened the hell out of me—imagine, giving a book like that to a poor little kid without a word of explanation. I used to jerk off quite a bit in bed at night when she'd gone out to have some fun. For a long time I couldn't get the hang of it, then, when I made it, when I had my first erection, when this stuff shot out all over the place, I was terrified. I thought it was brain fluid."

James stirred in his sleeping bag. "It probably was," he said softly.

I was wishing The Shadow would go, but I knew he wouldn't. The Capsellas could never get rid of him. I felt irritated with the pair of them, dropping off to sleep and leaving their horrible friend wandering around the house. The annoyance was so sharp in me that I said straight out, "I think it's time you went home."

Surprisingly, The Shadow agreed. He rose from his beanbag and began buttoning up his Burberry. I was amazed. It was so easy; obviously the Capsellas had never thought of anything so simple: You just told him to go, and he went. I even began to feel a little sorry for him, going off on his own to his empty apartment, and I walked with him to the door so he wouldn't feel neglected. As we passed through the living room I saw Mr. Capsella sound asleep on the sofa. The sight livened The Shadow a little.

"Does your dad often sleep on the sofa?" he pried.

"No," I said, "only when he's bor— I mean, only when he's tired out."

I saw him off to his car. He took a while starting the thing up; it was an old Plymouth with dents in the side. The Shadow never looked in his rearview mirror while he was driving; he said it made him paranoid. As the motor groaned into life I turned to go, but The Shadow called me back. He wound down the window and asked where the 7-Eleven was.

"It's in Box Hill," I said.

He drove off. As I watched the Plymouth out of sight, I congratulated myself: I'd figured out how to manage The Shadow. You just had to think of him as someone much younger than yourself: You gave him simple, direct instructions in a firm voice and he obeyed, and if he didn't, then you scared him a bit.

Back inside, James and Louis were wide awake. They had the same idea I'd had—that The Shadow, although he was so ancient looking, seemed much younger than we were.

"How old do you think he really is?" asked Louis.

We figured it out. He'd been a bit annoyed when I'd suggested his school days were thirty years back. He'd said twenty; that would make him thirty-five. There was no way he could be thirty-five, unless he had some kind of wasting disease. He was at least forty.

"I'm not going to be like that when I'm forty," vowed Louis. "I'm not even like that now." He blushed slightly; I suppose he was recalling the double-chin business.

It was weird. Before The Shadow had appeared, we'd all been feeling sorry for ourselves; we'd felt we had all kinds of things wrong with us. Now we seemed really sane and normal, even grown-up. It was a good feeling.

"He thinks about himself all the time," said Louis. Straightaway we decided not to be like that anymore; it was dangerous—it could become a lifetime habit.

"Do you think he's crazy?" asked James.

I'd once asked Mrs. Capsella this same question. She'd become quite cross about it; she seemed to imply that The Shadow wasn't nice enough to go insane, that the cases locked away in loony bins were a better class of people altogether. They had real problems, she said. The Shadow made his up.

"But they seem real to him," I'd said. And that was true, in a way. It was a bit like my fear of having heart attacks: You knew it wouldn't really happen, but you worried all the same. It took up *space* in your life; if you did it too much, there wouldn't be space left for better things. You might end up like The Shadow, forty-five years old and afraid to go to Box Hill, when Box Hill was just a simple, ordinary suburb with shops and houses and people walking around the streets.

"He's just a creep," said James.

"He's lonely," I said. "His wife ran away."

"She was probably a nice person."

"He's lonely because he's a creep," said Louis.

I said I thought he might be a creep because he was lonely.

"But he must have been a creep in the first place," argued James, "to *get* himself lonely. It's as simple as that: People ran off because he was a creep and got on their nerves."

"Broadside Williams is a creep," I said, "and he's not lonely."

"That's a different *kind* of creep," said Louis. "A sensible one."

We argued about it for a long time, all through the Thunderbirds, while it started getting light outside, and the birds began, and the bells of St. Matthews rang through the rain.

6 LAST THURSDAY, after classes, I tried to get into the school library. The library is the province of Dr. Spinner, a very learned lady, the only teacher in our school who has a Ph.D.: It's in Library Science from the University of Northern Colorado.

I needed a certain book badly: I had to find out the colors of the Bayeux Tapestry. The assignment was due on Monday, and I hadn't even begun. It wasn't that I hadn't thought about the subject; ever since Mossy Crocket handed the project out three weeks back, the thing had been haunting my head like a ghost. I brooded about it on Saturday afternoons, when I was hanging around the neighborhood with Louis and James, and on Sunday mornings while I watched the football replays. When I lay down to sleep at nights, the Bayeux horses came riding through my head, and I couldn't get my rest. Yet somehow I couldn't make a start on it; my mind seemed oddly paralyzed. I began wishing I was one of those kids who do their homework at school during first period and never waste a thought on it beforehand.

The Bayeux Tapestry project was just the kind of assignment Mossy Crocket loves. She's a bit of a loss as a history teacher; I don't think she really likes the subject very much at all. Whenever she takes a history book out of her brief-case, she seems faintly puzzled, as if she doesn't quite know what it is or why she has it with her. As she opens the covers and riffles through the pages, her face seems sad and she sighs. She only appears to like the pictures; she devotes whole periods to Art and Costume and Craft. She's always hanging around the art room, talking to Miss Mandel, and she wears clothes like Miss Mandel: hessian skirts and hand-woven smocks, red stockings and homemade plaited-leather shoes. But Mossy is a lot older than her arty friend—so old that no one knows why she's called Mossy; she's been at the school so long that the kids who gave her the name are probably grandparents now.

It's obvious to all of us that Mossy should have been an art teacher. I can easily picture her in her youth as one of Mrs. Capsella's romantic characters, a pale, slight girl with a name like Flora or Jessica and a savage old father called Colonel Crocket, who wouldn't allow his daughter to go to art school because he thought she'd get into loose com-pany.

Mossy's arty streak means that we all dread her assign-ments. When she came into the room that morning three weeks back, with her face lit up and her eyes moist and shining, we held our breath. She opened her shoulder bag dramatically and drew forth a mass of smudgy squares of gray paper. She'd photocopied a large print of the Bayeux Tapestry, then cut it up into little strips so that there was a piece for each of us. The idea was that you copied your piece, making it larger by using the scale she'd printed in the lefthand corner, and then when all the bits were handed in, Mossy would have a frieze to pin up in the school hall on Parent-Teacher Night.

"Make sure to use the right colors," she said.

James put his hand up. "Don't think I'm whining, Miss Crocket," he began, "but these photocopies are in black-and-white."

Mossy Crocket replied that she knew they were. She took up a big book she had on her desk and showed us a colored print of the tapestry, passing the book around the class. Everyone wanted to borrow it. Mossy turned pink and said uneasily, "I'm afraid that won't be possible; it's a school library book and it's overdue. I have to take it back this morning. Right after class, in fact." She looked at her watch.

There was a dead silence: It had begun the moment she said the words "school library."

"I'm sorry," Mossy apologized. She added unconvincingly, "You'll probably be able to get it out again, if—um—if you're nice."

"Being nice doesn't help," said Broadside Williams sternly. "I'm nice, but I've never been able to get a book out of the school library."

Mossy Crocket blushed deeper, as if it were her fault. "Well, Broad— I mean Gerald," she said, "you'll have to try harder." And then she remembered something that unlike most of our teachers, she often forgot, that she was the teacher and we were the kids. She said firmly: "And that means *all* of you," and went on to give a passable imitation of the kind of lecture we were hearing rather frequently these days: how at the high-school level we should be taking greater pains to research our assignments. "And if you find the school facilities inadequate in any way," she continued, then halted, and fell to blushing all over again, and her last words came out in a hasty whisper—"You should try the local public library."

She looked at her watch again, then out of the window, across the playground toward the library. We followed her glance. The library door was open. It was five minutes before the bell. "I'm leaving a little early today," Mossy said. No need to say why—we all guessed where she was headed. It was eleven o'clock: That book was an hour overdue. We watched her little figure trotting across the playground. We watched her mount the library steps, and as she reached the top one, the door closed. No one laughed; it was a humiliation familiar to all of us. Mossy didn't bother to knock; she knew the futility of it; she simply turned and walked back down again.

As she reached the bottom, Mr. Tweedie appeared, flustered and hurrying, a great load of books bundled awkwardly in his skinny arms. "No luck?" he asked Mossy, glancing upward toward the closed door. She shook her head mournfully; their shoulders drooped dispiritedly as they walked away in the direction of the staff room.

The library hours are set out in the school handbook and displayed on the brass plaque beside the library door. Ten A.M. to twelve P.M. for staff, one P.M. to two P.M. and three P.M. to five P.M. for students. But Dr. Spinner doesn't pay much attention to other peoples' timetables, and mostly you might say the library is closed. Dr. Spinner hasn't gone home though; if you look through the windows, you can see her, dusting and rearranging her books and glancing inside to see that no harm has come to them.

Dr. Spinner is mad about books, though in an entirely different way from the Capsellas. They're mad about reading books; Dr. Spinner is mad about keeping them in order. She's the kind of librarian who believes that libraries are for books, and people have no business there. She doesn't like people to take books out, or even to take them off the shelves and look inside. If you can get into the library, then Dr. Spinner will follow you all around it; this attention isn't kindly, she doesn't want to help you find what you're looking for, it's meant to scare you off. She stands up close beside you and says, "Have you found what you're looking for?" And whatever you answer—"Yes" or "No" or "Not yet"—she makes no reply, but simply stands there, dead quiet, getting on your nerves. She's tall and thin and very, very silent. She wears a hair net and gumshoes. Naturally there are clothes in between, but most of us would be hard put to describe them, even though teacher fashion is a prime subject of classroom gossip. We're too scared to look.

Dr. Spinner divides people into two classes: users and nonusers. Users are people who come into libraries and touch books; nonusers are those who stay outside. I once heard Broadside Williams telling one of his dim sex-jokes to a seventh grader he'd caught outside the shower block. The joke goes: "Is Dr. Spinner married to a user or a nonuser?" When you say, "I don't know," Broadside replies, "A nonuser."

"Why?"

"Because no one would want to use 'er."

The seventh grader didn't get it—he was one of those very small kids who start high school when they're ten and a half—and when Broadside saw the puzzled, worried expression on his face, he let him off without a detailed explanation.

Dr. Spinner's ambition is to turn the users into nonusers: simply, harmless people who leave books alone. She has several methods: One is to close the library. Behind the glass panel in the door, she's inserted a little ticket, green one side and pink the other. It's nicely printed, though not as fine as Mossy's printing (Mossy's is art; Dr. Spinner's looks like computer type). On the green side the print reads OPEN and on the pink it says CLOSED. Dr. Spinner's desk is beside a window next to the door, so she has a good sweeping view of the steps and all the approaches to the building. When there's no one about, the ticket is green, but as soon as a user approaches, the card flips around to pink.

And if you do get in and are brave enough to risk Dr. Spinner's silent, serpentine stare, even to walk ahead of her gumshoes and take a book from the shelves and proudly bear it to the desk for stamping, then you have to wait while she consults her "Notes on Offenders," a file she keeps on users, on simple people who've brought books back late or haven't paid their fines. Some names are printed in red: These are the folk who've left user marks on the pages, pencil marks or drops of tomato sauce or turned-down corners.

Once, years ago, before Dr. Spinner came out from America and got her iron grip on the place, there were kids in the school who used to cut out certain prints from the art books: paintings with nude men and women—probably nonusers—lounging around in grassy places. Dr. Spinner, fresh from Colorado and the higher realms of Library Science, found a solution to that problem in a jiffy: She went through all the art books with her rubber stamp and printed the school crest on all the bare breasts and backsides and other private parts she could find. No one bothers to cut prints out anymore, except for Broadside Williams, who says he likes tattooed women.

I didn't get in on Thursday afternoon. I hadn't really expected to, even though I crept along the back of the little garden beneath the windows instead of crossing the open playground. Dr. Spinner must have been watching: the card flipped over just as I jumped out from behind a large, serviceable rhododendron and landed square in the middle of the top step. Remembering Mossy's advice, I went on down to the public library in Blaxland Place, pausing at a phone booth to ring Mrs. Capsella and tell her I'd be late, so she wouldn't begin to fret about child molesters. As the coin dropped into the slot, I thought that if I had all the twenty-cent pieces I'd wasted on Mrs. Capsella's Bunny Lake Is Missing complex, I'd be a rich man.

The walk to the public library, like the twenty-cent piece, was wasted. The Art History section was as bare as Mother Hubbard's cupboard: others—lots of them—had gotten there first. I turned to the librarians behind the desk: They were friendly, cheerful souls, the kind of librarians you might see in a picture book, where the butcher is always a bold, rosy-cheeked fellow in a striped apron and the policeman a helmeted lad in a blue uniform who helps old ladies across the road. One librarian was plump and motherly, the other long and flat like a bookmark. I asked them if they knew what colors were used in the Bayeux Tapestry. They said they didn't know; someone had cut out the plates from the reference books.

"A lot of people have been in here with that question," the Bookmark added vaguely. I noticed she used the word "people" rather than "users," even when she was talking about the anti-social ones who'd taken the plates away. "It's a pity we don't have an answer for you," said the chubby one. The Bookmark said that she had a vague impression of green and gold, but that might have been a film she'd seen about King Arthur and his knights. Their ignorance seemed human, even touching. Nobody ever asked Dr. Spinner a question, but I'm sure if they did, she'd know the answer.

All I could recall from the print Mossy had shown us in class was a kind of multi-hued smudge. No one in our class knew. The kids in the other class knew all right—they'd got to the public library first—but they weren't telling.

So I decided to tackle Dr. Spinner again on Friday. There was one particular time when the library was almost always open: It was the ten A.M. time slot, which fell during first period, when all the kids and most of the teachers had classes and Dr. Spinner felt safe. She studied the timetable like a battle plan: There was a big copy pinned on the wall behind her desk, with big red ticks on the periods when everyone was occupied. We had Algebra first period, and I asked Mr. Tweedie if I could have ten minutes off to slip across to the library. He was most understanding and said, "I'd take twenty if I were you."

As I turned to go, he began fishing in his bag and called

me back. He had three books in his hands and a rather shifty, pleading expression in his eyes. "Could you return these for me?" he asked.

Stress made me turn nasty. "I hope they're not overdue," I said sternly.

"Three days early," he smiled proudly.

As I'd expected, getting inside the library was easier than usual. Dr. Spinner, off guard at that time, had deserted her watch post by the window and was browsing about the card catalogue. Though shocked to see me, she recovered at once and slid silently toward the desk. I put Mr. Tweedie's books down before her, and she seized them, turning at once to the back page to check on the date stamp. There was a queer, tense expectancy on her face, like a kid opening promising Christmas presents. She seemed quite certain she was going to get a good one, and her certainty unnerved me a little. Perhaps Mr. Tweedie's books *were* overdue; he wasn't a bad fellow, not the kind to play a dirty trick on me, but fear of Dr. Spinner could easily cause a minor change in personality.

"They're not mine," I said treacherously. "They're Mr. Tweedie's."

"They may not be yours," said Dr. Spinner in a low, menacing tone. "But neither are they Mr. Tweedie's. They are the property of Lawson High School." The menace was slightly tinged with disappointment. Mr. Tweedie's books had proved clean as a whistle.

I kept quiet; I needed that book for my assignment. I nodded politely and even smiled a little cravenly as I backed away from the desk and began moving cautiously in the direction of the bookshelves. There was a soft padding sound as Dr. Spinner followed in her gumshoes, but I didn't turn my head. As I searched along the shelves, I was aware of her looming just behind my left shoulder, the place where evil spirits are supposed to stand.

I found the Bayeux Tapestry book right away. It was an amazing testimony to Dr. Spinner's strength of character: at least forty kids were desperate to get their hands on that book, and it still stood safe upon the shelves, right where it was supposed to be. A place for everything and everything in its place. For some odd reason an image of the crazy lady in the off-peak electricity ad flashed into my mind.

"Have you found what you are looking for?" asked Dr. Spinner. She knew I had—that's why she asked. The question really meant, "Are you still going to take that book off the shelves while I am looking at you?" It is amazing how creepy that particular kind of low, slow voice can be—for some reason it always reminds me of screaming, though no one had ever heard Dr. Spinner scream. Unlike most of the teachers in our establishment, she has no need to.

I turned and found myself staring at her mouth. Once I saw a lady at a concert who reminded me strongly of Dr. Skinner; she was playing a clarinet in the orchestra. At first I couldn't figure out the resemblance; the musician was quite pretty, even gentle in appearance. Then it clicked: The likeness was in the mouth. When the lady blew on her clarinet, her lips puckered in a hard, ugly shape. Dr. Skinner's mouth looked like that, only it didn't have a clarinet in it.

Suddenly I felt a surge of anger against her, the way she

scared everybody and kept the place shut up like a monument. I shifted my gaze from her mouth and looked her straight in the eye like a snake charmer. "Yes, I've found what I was looking for," I said firmly. "And now I'm going to take it out."

She didn't flinch. She followed me across to her desk and drew out her "Notes on Offenders." Although I'd paid all my fines, her confident manner disturbed me a little, and I opened my book and began hastily memorizing the colors.

"Close that book at once and attend to me," snapped Dr. Spinner.

I attended.

"You had an overdue book in last week."

"Only half a day overdue. And I paid the fine."

She smiled at me. It was awful. "I know," she said.

"So I don't see what's the matter."

"There's a new rule."

I said I hadn't heard about any new rule. "I don't get in here much," I added meaningfully. "None of us do." I expected she'd be angry at this remark, but she seemed downright pleased; for a moment I thought she was going to break down and chuckle. Instead, she explained the new rule. It was just what you'd expect: Anyone with one overdue book a month was barred from using the library for two weeks. I handed the book over and went on my way. As I reached the door she asked me to flip the card over to CLOSED as I went out. "It's twelve o'clock," she said. It was nowhere near that hour. Dr. Spinner's watch, like its owner, kept special time.

7 THERE WAS ANOTHER, more personal reason for worrying about this particular assignment of Mossy Crocket's. I couldn't draw. I never have been able to. As I filled sheet after sheet of Mrs. Capsella's typing paper with drawings that would have brought shame on a disabled first grader, I was vastly annoyed with Mossy. After all, this was supposed to be a history assignment, and I was quite good at history; I'd been hoping to get an A this year. But because I couldn't draw, I wouldn't have a hope, and it was all Mossy's fault—for being arty and wearing colored stockings and hopsack and not being brave enough to defy her military father and go to art school.

As the assignment wasn't fair anyway, it seemed excusable to get a little help from the Capsellas. It wasn't the night for approaching Mr. Capsella; he was lounging in the television room, watching *The Golden Years of Hollywood* and looking depressed. There was an enormous pile of essays on the coffee table beside him; he'd begin marking them at two A.M., and until then he was better left to brood alone. Besides, I knew from previous experience exactly what would happen if I approached him with my assignment: He'd bring out every history book in the house and make me look through all of them. When I'd finished that, he'd treat me to an exhaustive lecture on medieval art. And if I told him it was just a simple matter of copying a drawing to scale and coloring it in correctly, he wouldn't believe me; he wouldn't believe anyone in the teaching profession could be so silly.

Then there was the little matter of the assignment being due the very next day. If he discovered this, it would stir up all kinds of grievances. First, he'd become sadly reminiscent: He'd drone on about how studious and eager he'd been as a boy, how he'd always handed in essays days early, and how necessary it was to develop desirable work habits when one was young. Then he'd become depressed about my future, picturing me as a used-car salesman or a city worker, which was a polite term he used for garbage collector. At such times I often felt tempted to tell him that being a garbage collector wasn't a bad job; the hours were good and so was the money, it was outdoor work, and you'd get a fine tan even in winter. And there's always garbage around, so you'd never be out of a job. But I never did tell him, because his grim visions of my future always made him so sad looking, I feared he might cry.

I sneaked past his door and entered Mrs. Capsella's study. She was seated at her desk, slouched over a sheet of paper, a glum expression on her face. Even from the doorway I could see that the sheet of paper was blank, and that there were a lot of screwed-up scribbled-over ones tossed around the floor at her feet. She was having a bad night. Without even turning around to see if it was me or Mr. Capsella, she yelled, "I'm not making any cooked suppers: If you're hungry, get yourselves some toast."

"It's my homework," I explained in a small, pathetic voice. She turned around then all right, and I watched her face grow pale. I knew what the matter was: She was afraid it was English homework. Essays like "Why Do Birds Fly South in Winter?" and "Never Have I Felt Such Cold" frightened her badly.

"It's all right," I reassured her. "It's History." I showed her the photocopy. "We have to draw it again," I explained, "in scale."

Mrs. Capsella peered at the smudgy paper, her forehead crinkling up into little ridges that made her look a hundred. "Mmm," she said. Then she fell silent. Her hands, on the desk, appeared lifeless. I knew this ploy: She didn't like the look of the assignment and was hoping if she kept quiet, I'd go away. It was rather like a mouse playing dead.

I didn't intend to go away; she was my last hope—she'd won a prize for drawing in primary school.

"You know I can't *draw*," I whined in my small, pathetic voice, and went on a little about the unfairness of giving out drawing assignments in History—not too much though, in case she went down to the school to complain.

"Oh, all *right*," she said sulkily when I'd finished. She stared into my face. "You look tired. Lie down on the sofa and have a rest."

I passed her the box of Magic Markers. "I *think* the colors are yellow and—"

"Oh, never mind about the *colors*—"

"But—"

"Just *rest*."

I rested.

Twenty minutes later I had to get up and see how she

was progressing. The sighs and irritable exclamations and, more ominously, the occasional burst of jolly humming were worrying me. I looked over her shoulder. What I saw horrified me. The horses were queer, misshapen: great big heads with enormous fish eyes, bulbous bodies, skinny little legs that wouldn't have supported a row of anemic fox terriers.

I should have known better: This was the conclusion forced upon me every time the Capsellas helped me with my homework, yet I never seemed to learn from the experience.

"I thought you got a prize for drawing when you were at school," I said rather pettishly.

Producing those misbegotten ponies and filling in the suits of armor with a pattern of fish scales had made Mrs. Capsella irritable. "That was for drawing ballet dancers," she snapped. "And I was only nine."

I couldn't complain further; it would seem like ingratitude. Besides, she hadn't done the bottom part. This was the smudgiest piece of the photocopy—a mysterious litter that resembled Elwood Beach on a summer's night when everyone had gone home. I knew that Broadside Williams, if he bothered to do the assignment at all, would fill it in with Fosters cans and battered cigarette packs, perhaps even the odd contraceptive.

"What do you think that part's meant to be?" I asked.

"Search me," replied Mrs. Capsella bluntly. She put her head on one side and considered for a moment. "A floral border?" she suggested.

"What?"

"You know—leaves and flowers, that sort of thing." Before I could stop her, she'd picked up a Magic Marker and filled in a row of tulips, the kind you see pinned up on the walls of kindergartens, titled *Spring in Holland*.

"I don't think it would have been *tulips*," I said.

"Now, look!" screeched Mrs. Capsella. "Don't blame *me*! If you wanted it exactly right, then you should have looked it up properly in the library!"

The whole business had unnerved me—I wailed like a kid, "Dr. Spinner wouldn't let me!"

"What?"

I found myself telling her the whole story. It was just the kind of tale she loved to hear.

"Well!" she cried, deeply thrilled. Then she began asking all kinds of questions, most of them irrelevant or inexplicable: what kind of clothes Dr. Spinner wore, what her husband was like, whether she had children, whether she stayed away from school very often. I didn't know the answers to all these questions; I didn't even know if Dr. Spinner had a husband. I told her Broadside Williams's joke—the one about whether Dr. Spinner's husband was a user or a nonuser. I shouldn't have wasted my breath; Mrs. Capsella is dumb about jokes.

"What do you mean, 'use her'?" she asked. "Do you mean the husband was a person who didn't like libraries, so he didn't—"

"Oh, don't worry about it," I said hastily. "It's not a good joke—you know Broadside Williams."

"He's quite a nice boy," said Mrs. Capsella unexpectedly. Most of the parents thought Broadside Williams should get himself seen to. Then she returned to the joke, worrying at it like a dog with an unwieldy bone. To distract her, I described Dr. Skinner's gumshoes, her hair net and her low, scary voice. I mentioned the Ph.D. from the University of Northern Colorado.

These details excited Mrs. Capsella so much that she dragged out some fresh paper and began scribbling notes. She filled the first sheet up quickly, then two more, humming to herself all the time. Her absorption worried me; she might be planning something.

"Don't go up to the school," I pleaded. "Don't go near the library."

"Gosh, no," said Mrs. Capsella. "I wouldn't dare."

I could hardly believe my ears. "Really?"

Mrs. Capsella gave a shy smile. "I'm scared of librarians," she confided. "They're strange people. Did you know that Dewey, the man who invented decimal cataloging, was nearly eaten by a dog when he was two years old?"

I frowned. "That doesn't mean he was strange—just because a dog bit him."

"Dogs *know*," said Mrs. Capsella mysteriously. She picked up her pen and returned to her scribbling.

"You're not writing a letter to the school, are you?"

"Oh, no, just notes."

"Why?"

"Well, they might come in handy somewhere or other."

"Don't write a story about Dr. Spinner for the *Women's Weekly*," I cried.

Mrs. Capsella turned shifty. She didn't answer exactly; she didn't promise she wouldn't. She said airily, "Oh, you don't have to worry about that. Librarians don't read the *Women's Weekly*."

"They might. The ones at the public library do; I've seen it on their desk."

"But not ones with doctorates from Northern Colorado. They read things like *Library Trends* and *Aslib Proceedings.*"

I wasn't convinced.

"You'd better go to bed," Mrs. Capsella advised. "It's twelve thirty. Don't *worry*," she added as I trailed wearily to the door.

But I couldn't sleep at all that night. It wasn't just anxiety. The Capsellas kept me awake: Mrs. Capsella humming and scratching behind the wall like a singing mouse in a cozy hole, Mr. Capsella shuffling his essay papers, throwing pens against the wall and grouching to himself about illiterates. I don't think his students had acquired desirable work habits when they were young, or perhaps they'd had school librarians like Dr. Spinner and had never been able to get their hands on a book.

As it turned out, I needn't have worried about Mrs. Capsella coming to the school to get a look at Dr. Spinner. On Monday there was a special announcement at morning assembly, which, as usual, was held in the bleakest part of the school yard. The headmaster delivered it. He was known as King Arthur—it was in fact his real name; his parents had christened him Kingsley Raymond Arthur. We all used the shorter version: It suited him, for he was a man of majestic stature, with red hair and beard. He looked like a giant from an old storybook, or an ax murderer from a modern one.

During the previous night, he told us, some—here he paused; he'd started to say "vandals," but swiftly changed the word to "intruders"—some intruders had broken into the library. They hadn't smashed anything or done any real damage at all, they'd simply taken some books—again he paused. This time he'd been about to say "away"; now, with a smirk, he changed it to "out." At this there rose a muffled, ragged cheer that seemed to come from a little knot of teachers huddled for warmth about the incinerator. Dr. Spinner, King Arthur continued, had been badly shaken by the incident. In fact, she'd had a minor breakdown and would be away on sick leave for a few weeks, resting. He added in a more menacing tone that the person/persons responsible, when located, would be dealt with according to his/her/their merits.

"And given prizes," suggested Broadside Williams. He was given one himself: two lunch hours picking up papers from the school courtyard. Several of us helped him out; it was necessary as well as kindly, for he was too fat to bend over smoothly. He really needed one of those sticks with a spear point on the end that park keepers have in old English movies.

As we worked, we speculated on the form Dr. Spinner's minor breakdown might have taken. Teacher breakdowns were quite often announced at assembly, particularly toward the close of term. Sometimes the teachers came back, sometimes they didn't; sometimes they went to work at the correspondence school.

Broadside said he knew exactly what form Spinner's breakdown had taken; he had inside information. When King Arthur had rung her on Sunday night to break the news that her books had been tampered with, she'd walked straight out of her house and down the street, shedding her clothes as she went. Stark naked, she'd walked up the garden path of a perfect stranger, knocked on the door, and asked if she could take a bath. Broadside had gotten this information from his cousin, who happened to own the house with the door on which Dr. Spinner had knocked. The cousin had told him that without her clothes Dr. Spinner was a knockout. She had a tattoo on her chest which read, "I love Melvil Dewey."

I was surprised by this—not the tale itself, I knew he'd made it up—but the fact that Broadside Williams, who always seemed the perfect lout, had heard about Dewey. Sometimes I suspected he was a secret reader.

I related the incident to Mrs. Capsella, though I used King Arthur's official version rather than Broadside's more lurid tale. Mrs. Capsella didn't seem surprised. "Off to the correspondence school," she said, and added more kindly. "She'll like it there, the users are all a long way away."

"WEAR PROPER CLOTHES," I cautioned Mrs. Capsella on the evening of the Parent-Teacher
Night. I said it pleasantly, not wishing to get off
to a bad start by antagonizing her. Really, it
was her interests I had at heart; I didn't want her to walk
into the school hall in her biker outfit and find herself sadly
out of place, stared at by wiser mothers in neat checked
skirts and crew-neck sweaters and smart velvet blazers.

Even though I spoke with moderation, Mrs. Capsella still
took offense. She had a particular way of doing this: She
didn't get angry or tell you not to be smart; she simply
picked out one of your words and went on about it. In this
case it was "proper": She wanted to know what it meant.

I shuffled my feet a bit. When she took the word out of
the sentence like that and held it up for you to look at on
its own, it suddenly began to appear strange. I felt silly,
even snobbish, and found myself blushing uncomfortably.
"I just mean a nice dress or something," I muttered, "not
that biker outfit, not those old jeans and boots."

"A nice dress," echoed Mrs. Capsella wonderingly, as if
she'd never heard of such a thing.

"A checked skirt," I suggested helpfully, "and a jacket—
you know—like all the other mothers wear."

When I said "all the other mothers," Mrs. Capsella frowned.

She closed her eyes as if she were going to take a little nap in the hallway, standing on her feet like a horse. I suppose she was only thinking, for in a moment she opened her eyes again and said slowly, "Amazing, isn't it?"

I blushed. I thought she was referring to miserable ingratitude, brooding on the fact that I, her own son, was criticizing her clothes and telling her how to dress.

"You don't want them all staring at you," I said weakly. I should have known better: Mrs. Capsella never really notices people staring. When she walks up to the drugstore without any shoes, and the ladies busy in their gardens say, "Don't you feel cold?" Mrs. Capsella can't think why they should ask such a question; she stands there looking puzzled and answers, "No, I've got my coat on."

"What's amazing?" I asked uneasily.

Mrs. Capsella put her head on one side. "Those checked skirts and velvet jackets. I was coming home from Dasher's place the other day and I noticed that every woman in the bus was wearing them, and the checked skirts were all red and the jackets were all navy blue." She leaned toward me. "Why do you think they all do it?"

I shrugged. "I suppose it's normal," I said.

"I think it's bloody abnormal," said Mrs. Capsella frankly, "And I'm not having any of it."

"But—"

She ignored my interruption. "It's interesting in a way," she reflected. "Actually, I think I've figured out why they do it."

I listened patiently while she expounded a theory she'd

made up to account for normal ladies wearing normal clothes. It had nothing to do with fashion, and much to do with the kind of psychology she and Dasher invented on rainy afternoons. When women reached a certain age, she explained, they looked in the mirror and decided to become invisible.

"Why would they want to make themselves invisible?"

"Perhaps because they are bullied by their teenage sons," replied Mrs. Capsella meaningfully. I ignored the meaningfulness, and she went on: "So then they go to some overpriced store and buy checked shirts and velvet blazers and wear them forever after." She added, "I haven't quite reached that stage." She gazed at me thoughtfully. "All the same, I understand how you feel. When I was a kid, I used to be embarrassed by Aunt Rowdy. She was really old—or she seemed so to me; I suppose she couldn't have been more than fifty at the time—and she used to wear colored plastic bands in her hair, the kind with little specks of silver glitter in them. And white sand-shoes and tennis socks."

"At least she had something on her feet," I said coldly, meaningful in my turn.

"I always wear shoes when I go out," replied Mrs. Capsella. "Except when I go to the drugstore, and that doesn't count, because it's in the neighborhood."

I sighed.

"Poor thing," said Mrs. Capsella. "It's difficult having a Visible Mother. I won't wear the biker outfit. I'll wear a dress."

"Not from the thrift shop," I pleaded. I was particularly nervous because she and Dasher had spent the previous day touring thrift shops in Dasher's beat-up VW. They'd brought back a vanfull of tacky satin blouses and spent the evening cutting the sleeves off and sewing feathers around the armholes. They'd lopped off the buttons as well, and replaced them with leather boot laces. The finished products were called Disco Jerkins, and Dasher planned to sell them at Camberwell Market on Sunday. I felt Mrs. Capsella was quite capable of wearing one to the Parent-Teacher Night just to drum up a little business for her friend.

"Some of those thrift-shop dresses have very good labels: They're models."

I didn't reply. Normally I'd have answered "Real vintage models," but I didn't want to push my luck when she was beginning to show signs of reason. Instead I offered to help her go through her wardrobe. She did have some decent clothes; Mr. Capsella bought them hopefully for her birthdays. I found them all pushed to the back, with their cardboard tickets still attached. I drew one out; a gray dress with little buttons down the back, neat little buttons covered with the same cloth as the dress.

Mrs. Capsella made a face when she saw it. "Gray makes me look yellow," she complained.

I took out a smart black pleated skirt.

"Too dowdy," she cried.

There were similar remarks about every decent garment I found: They were all dowdy or else invisible, the colors were wrong or the material gave her a rash. She lay at her ease on the bed, watching me drag things out and put them back again, saying, "No, I don't think so," all the time.

Then she had an idea. "Let's look in the hall cupboard," she said. "There's a lot of clothes in there."

I wasn't hopeful. The hall cupboard was the place where the Capsellas stored all the things they'd grown tired of: Mr. Capsella's home-handyman books and print developing set, Mrs. Capsella's contraptions for making bean curd and growing alfalfa sprouts. There were shelves full of tangled balls of wool and unfinished garments from the time before Mrs. Capsella had discovered that knitting gave you brain damage, and at the bottom, in deep cardboard boxes, all the clothes she'd worn in her youth and never had the heart to throw out: miniskirts and leopard-print blouses and a terrible sheepskin coat with big flowers embroidered all around the edges in colored wools.

"Another hippy coat," I shuddered.

This nettled Mrs. Capsella. "I wish you wouldn't keep saying I was a hippie," she cried, "because I never was." She flung the coat to one side and made a grab at something else. "Oh, look!" she breathed.

I looked. It was a dress, quite a nice one, blue silky stuff with little white flowers printed all over it.

"The last time I wore this," said Mrs. Capsella, "was when I went out with Leonard Cuttle."

"Did you go out with Leonard Cuttle?" I asked. I could hardly believe it. Leonard Cuttle was a tiny quiet man who worked in Mr. Capsella's department at the University. He was so small and quiet that if the University had closed down, he could easily have found a job as a gnome in someone's front garden.

"Isn't he ghastly?" giggled Mrs. Capsella unfeelingly. Then she blushed. "I don't mean how he looks," she added hastily. "It was just that he was awfully stingy in those days; you knew that if you went out with him, you'd have to walk miles, because he wouldn't pay a bus fare and he wouldn't let you pay either."

"Why did you go out with him, then?"

"I didn't like to refuse in case he thought it was because of the way he looked. You have to go if someone as small as that asks you out."

"Really?" I said. I couldn't imagine any of the girls in our school thinking along those lines. If they didn't like the look of you, they'd simply tell you to get lost. "Did you have to walk a long way?"

"Well, no. The cinema was on the harbor. You had to go by ferry, and he couldn't swim."

I couldn't tell if she was joking or not. "What was it like—the, um, evening?" I was curious; whenever Mrs. Capsella met Leonard Cuttle, she always behaved as though she'd never seen him before, and he acted the same with her. Mr. Capsella always had to introduce them.

"Awful," sighed Mrs. Capsella.

"How?"

"I can't remember, really. I was so bored, I must have blacked out or something. All I can really recall is sneaking off the ferry at Cremorne Point, when he thought I was in the ladies' room, and catching a taxi home." She paused, then went on reflectively, "He thought I'd fallen overboard. He never asked me out again."

No wonder, I thought. Aloud I said, "It would have been better if you'd said you didn't want to go out in the first place. You always go on about how people should say what they think."

"Mmm," said Mrs. Capsella vaguely, as she always did when you caught her with something.

She tried on the dress, humming to herself. As I've said, it was a nice dress, and it fit all right, and it wasn't too young or anything. She raked out some tights and high-heeled shoes to go with it, and even tried a little makeup. I can't tell you how different she seemed. It was queer, all wrong; she reminded me of the drawings you find in old fairy-tale books: the wolf dressed up as Red Riding Hood's grandmother, sinister and unconvincing in his frilly cap and knitted shawl, ready to leap out of bed and eat people up. I imagined the surprise on my friends' faces, and on the teachers', when they saw her got up like this. They'd think something had happened to her; they might think she'd had a religious conversion, that she'd become a Je-hovah's Witness or even a Mormon. I thought I'd hated the biker outfit and the thrift-shop models, but there was no doubt about it; somehow those things suited her. They were normal for her. I couldn't think how to tell her this; she'd gone to such a lot of trouble and she seemed so pleased with herself, humming and dancing about in front of the mirror.

Mr. Capsella saved the day; he came through the door-way and stared at Mrs. Capsella cavorting in the blue dress. He seemed stunned. "What's happened?" he cried. "Has your mother died?"

Mrs. Capsella shot him a scornful glance and began un-buttoning the dress in a cross kind of way. It was clear she found both of us oppressive and unreasonable. "There's no pleasing some people," she said, tossing the blue dress on the floor and crossing to the wardrobe to hunt out her biker outfit.

9 IT WAS A BEAUTIFUL EVENING as we set out for the Parent-Teacher Night. At least this is what the Capsellas said, and I suppose they were right; I was too apprehensive to care all that much about the weather. The sky was very black and the stars were very bright, and there was warmth in the air and a smell of damp grass and flowers. It reminded you of summer coming and everything that went with summer: long light evenings and crickets in the alley behind the drugstore, cicadas singing and frogs croaking in the creek in the reserve.

The Capsellas found the night so beautiful, they decided to walk to school.

"But you can't," I cried.

"Why not?" asked Mr. Capsella, frowning slightly. He wasn't all that crazy about Parent-Teacher Nights; they made him tense. The teachers' remarks on my progress depressed him in the same way that thinking about tree roots getting under the foundations did; at such times I suspected him of considering me a bad investment.

"Yes, why not?" echoed Mrs. Capsella.

I explained patiently that parents didn't walk to Parent-Teacher Night; they went in cars. If you wanted to take a walk, then you did it on Sunday afternoons, along the jogging tracks in the reserve.

"And I suppose you wear Adidas tracksuits," said Mrs. Capsella scornfully.

Mr. Capsella stood on the pavement with a puzzled expression on his face. He didn't know what we were talking about; he honestly didn't have a clue. "What does Adidas mean?" he asked.

He was like that. His head was so full of learning that there wasn't much room for anything else, and it took him a while to figure out the meaning of any little incident that occurred in the real world. Because of the slight uncertainty this gave him, it was sometimes easy to push him around a little. You just had to be firm.

"Let's go in the car," I said purposefully; sure enough, he began to move toward it.

Mrs. Capsella seized him by the arm. "Come on," she said. "We'll walk. Al's just got a fit of the normals. He wants to be like everyone else, so we have to be exactly like everyone else's parents."

"How's that?" asked Mr. Capsella, quite unaware that he was using a cricketing term.

"That's how teenagers are these days," said Mrs. Capsella. "They don't want to be different; they want to be the same."

"I don't understand what that's got to do with walking," said Mr. Capsella.

"Don't worry about it," she replied, and began to drag him along the footpath. As they passed under a streetlight, I noticed that Mr. Capsella was wearing the striped sweater he'd bought at K Mart five years back: The stripes were orange and brown, and there was a row of beige snow-flakes around the chest. He loved that sweater; he wore it right through from April to November, except when it was at the dry cleaners, and then it seemed funny to see him without it, almost as if it wasn't a piece of clothing at all but part of his body, like an arm or a leg. I'd been too busy worrying about Mrs. Capsella to think about his clothes. I wouldn't have had a hope of getting him out of the sweater anyway.

The Capsellas walked slowly, pausing to sniff at bushes and look up at the sky. I skulked behind a little. At the corner of Wentworth Street, Mrs. Cadigorn drove up in her Volvo. She slowed down when she saw the Capsellas and poked her neat head out of the window. "Everything all right?" she asked. It was the kind of question normal people like Mrs. Cadigorn feel impelled to ask when they see people like the Capsellas. She was a kind lady; she probably thought their car had broken down and they were in need of a lift.

"Yes, thank you," answered Mrs. Capsella.

Mr. Capsella whispered something to her. I suppose he was wondering who Mrs. Cadigorn was, for Mrs. Capsella at once performed an introduction. Mr. Capsella smiled pleasantly and remarked that it was a beautiful evening. "Like Paradise," he added horribly, and I saw Mrs. Cadigorn's neat head give a little jerk of surprise. Then she recovered and asked if they'd like a lift.

"It's nice of you," said Mrs. Capsella, "but we like walking."

Mrs. Cadigorn didn't seem convinced, for she followed the Capsellas very slowly along the curb in her Volvo, like a policeman who is getting ready to take down a name and address. "Are you sure?" she persisted.

"We're looking at the stars," Mrs. Capsella informed her. Mrs. Cadigorn drove away then, and I was glad of it, because some moments later my parents began having a little difference of opinion.

Mrs. Capsella liked Parent-Teacher Nights; she loved talking to people, and she didn't get much opportunity to do this with the kind of job she had. She liked to arrive at the school hall late, around ten thirty or so, when the teachers were tired out and rather ratty; she said that then they'd tell you all kinds of interesting things they wouldn't dream of revealing at eight o'clock, before they'd lost their grip. Mr. Capsella didn't approve of this approach to my education; he thought it rather frivolous, and I heard him telling her now that the Parent-Teacher Night wasn't a social occasion or an opportunity to gather material for her work. He wanted to find out exactly how I was doing at school. Education, he said, was a serious business.

Mrs. Capsella was wounded by these remarks. As usual, she chose a word, and bothered him about it. The word was "serious," and she went on at some length, describing in detail just what a serious person she was at heart. Her interest in the teachers' private lives was serious as well, she insisted; she wanted to discover whether they had serious attitudes toward their serious profession. It was all a load of bullshit really: She just liked talking to people and gathering up little bits and pieces for her stories.

"I suppose *you're* going to ask them for the syllabus again," she remarked.

Mr. Capsella didn't reply.

"You won't get it," Mrs. Capsella said.

For three years Mr. Capsella has been trying to get copies of the syllabus from teachers. They never let him have it; they always make excuses: They say they don't have copies on them, or that there is no syllabus for their particular subject, or that they're not allowed to give it out to parents. If Mr. Capsella were a used-car salesman or a city worker, they'd be quite happy to oblige, snobbishly believing such people are morons who can't read small print. But because Mr. Capsella is a teacher of sorts, they think he's going to read it closely in order to check up on them. And though he's never yet succeeded in getting a look at anyone's syllabus, he never gives up: Every single Parent-Teacher Night he really believes he's going to find someone silly enough to hand one over. When he comes in the door, you can see the teachers exchanging glances with each other, sometimes their lips move as well, like bad ventriloquists: "Here comes the Syllabus Man," they're flashing to each other. In his own quiet, scholarly way, Mr. Capsella is almost as much a nuisance to me as Mrs. Capsella.

I try my best to keep a low profile at school, yet somehow I'm conspicuous. I blame the Capsellas for this: The staff room is a hive of gossip, with parents a favorite topic. I feel sure I'm known as "that queer Capsella woman's child" or even "Son of Syllabus Man." The repercussions of this are unfortunate: When every single person in our class is talking, there is hardly a teacher in the school who doesn't deal with the problem by saying, "Capsella, stop talking." Even when my mouth is actually closed, they still say it; a habit like that is hard to break. This is why I get such dubious reports on Parent-Teacher Night: It isn't that my marks are particularly low; it's just that the teachers feel they have to complain about someone whose father is always trying to get the syllabus. They have no real grievances about me, so they bring up talking in class; they imply that my marks would be better if I'd close my mouth for a moment. This is just the sort of comment that most disturbs Mr. Capsella and makes him return to the subject of desirable work habits. Mrs. Capsella has a different reaction to the teacher whines: She simply replies, "Does he?" and then, "But don't they all talk? I did—didn't you?" And though it's kind of her to take my part, such replies simply make me more conspicuous than ever.

The school hall was set out in a cheerless fashion. The teachers sat at little tables arranged around the edges of the room: They reminded you of stall holders at a fair, only they had nothing to sell except bad news. There was a line of chairs set down the middle of the hall, where the parents were supposed to sit while waiting for their interviews. Most of them were too nervous to sit down at all; they prowled around the hall or stood in fretful little clumps beside the teachers' tables, hoping to overhear bad news about someone else's kids. The men looked at their shoes, and the women looked at the other women's dresses and husbands.

The organization of the interviews was peculiar: The system had been invented a long time back, when the school had only two hundred students. Now it had eight hundred, but no one had changed the system because they couldn't figure out a new one to put in its place. The parents had a three-minute interview with each teacher; at the end of the three minutes a bell would ring, and they would go on to the next one on their list or sit down on the chairs to wait their turn. But because most of the parents had serious attitudes like Mr. Capsella and the teachers were dying to defend themselves and lay the blame on us, the interviews tended to run overtime. Before the first five interviews had finished, the whole thing had become rather like a badly overcrowded game of musical chairs, with the interview times all out of kilter and the parents racing for vacant teachers whenever the bell rang, pushing and shoving a bit, and whining to one another when they lost out.

It was fairly quiet when we arrived. There'd only been one or two interviews; the real hubbub hadn't begun. I separated myself from the Capsellas and went into the small kitchen at the back. Normally I wouldn't be caught dead at a Parent-Teacher Night, but I'd been chosen to serve the cups of coffee to those parents who were still capable of holding a cup and saucer. I hadn't been chosen because I was particularly polite or presentable or good at making coffee—it was just that I'd been too slow on my feet getting out of the room when King Arthur was looking for conscripts.

The five other slow runners were already in the kitchen: Sophie Disher and her friend Kelly Krake, James, who'd been with me when I got caught, and Oswald Padkin, a kid from the other class who's supposed to be a genius, the kind of kid I rather expect Mr. Capsella would consider a good investment. Oswald was a lot like Mr. Capsella— good at schoolwork, but a bit lost in the world. He's brainy all right, but not smart enough to realize that if you've got a name like Oswald, the thing to do is change it to something normal, like Ozzie. And you can't explain this to him either, because he's apt to shake all over when people talk to him, even if they make some perfectly harmless remark like "Have a good weekend?" He's small and white colored like a British person, and he's got frizzy pale hair, glasses, and big teeth. He looks exactly like the kids you find on the covers of books with titles like *The Wizard of Pont Street*, unlikely tales about brainy kids whom everybody hates until they invent a cure for rabies or a car engine that runs on seawater and make themselves and their schools famous. Then everybody's lining up to be their friend. Only it doesn't work like this in real life: If Oswald Padkin invented some wonder that put the school on the scientific map, he'd still be shaking like a leaf if anyone tried to say a word to him, and pretty soon people would stop trying.

Because of his scientific knowhow, and the greater reliability that this suggested to the teachers, Oswald was in charge of the stopwatch that timed the three-minute interviews: It gave him a good excuse to keep his head down and not look at anyone. He didn't have to say anything except "Now!" every three minutes, when it was time for Sophie Disher to ring the bell.

Sophie was Broadside Williams's girlfriend. Every time I saw her, I looked carefully (and I hope discreetly) to see if she'd started getting fat. I don't mean pregnant—though a lot of people were looking for that as well—I mean simple fat, putting on weight. I'd read somewhere that people who are married for a long time or even just see a lot of each other often start to look alike. This is just the kind of thing that fascinates me: It hadn't seemed to work in the Capsellas' case, and I was interested to see if it would work with Sophie Disher and Broadside Williams—whether Broadside would start getting thin, or Sophie fat, or if Sophie would stop being scared about growing fat, or Broadside begin to worry about his weight. They spent a lot of time together mooning about behind the shower block at lunchtime, and you always saw them lounging about outside the fish-and-chip shop on Friday and Saturday nights. I glanced discreetly at Sophie. She didn't seem different at all, except for a rather nasty case of ringworm on her neck.

Just then King Arthur appeared in the doorway, his face as red as his beard and his bright blue eyes looking hot and shiny and boiled. He was buttoned tightly into an unfamiliar and somewhat tasteless jacket of mustard-colored wool. The tastelessness probably wasn't his fault: He was so big, he had to buy his clothes at the Outsize Warehouse, and there wasn't all that much choice there. You could see how nervous he was, because the jacket armpits were soaked through. The hairy cloth must have been at least an inch thick. "Just keep ringing that bell," he ordered Sophie. "Every three minutes—no more, no less."

We began trundling out the coffee. There were cookies as well, teddy bears and clocks with pink icing on the back, two each on the saucers, getting damp. Most of the parents refused the cookies, and I didn't blame them; they were the cheapest kind you could buy, generic and they looked it. The coffee was generic too, but all coffee looks much the same in a cup; they wouldn't discover its true nature until they'd tasted it. All the stuff in our school cafeteria, and in the lavatories and shower block, was generic; if you could buy generic teachers, we'd have had them as well. Perhaps we did.

I glanced around the hall: There was quite a bit of absenteeism among the staff; lots of the tables were empty. The teachers hated Parent-Teacher Nights even more than we did, and some of them stayed away from school in the day as well, just to make their absence at night seem more convincing. The ones who came to school were so nervous, they couldn't give a proper lesson. Mr. Tweedie had spent the first half of the period complaining about our marks in the term exam, and the second half he'd spent telling us a long, soppy story about himself. The story was as soft as one of Mrs. Capsella's: One lunchtime Mr. Tweedie had gone into the staff room, frail and hungry and worn out, and had taken one bite of his sandwich when a kid appeared at the door wanting help with his algebra. Mr. Tweedie had left his sandwich—I'll bet it was gone when he got back—and spent the whole of the lunch hour helping the kid. He often did that kind of thing, he said, his voice trembling a little.

The funny thing about this story was that it was probably true: He would help you whenever you asked. It was just that his help didn't help. He was so smart, he couldn't imagine what it was like to have the kind of mind that couldn't understand algebra. He was as mystified by our idiocy as we were by matrices and vectors. You felt furious with him and sorry for him at the same time: The emotion was completely wasted; we kept on failing.

Algebra is an important subject; you need it for just about anything. I knew the parents wouldn't waste time feeling sorry for Mr. Tweedie; they'd just be furious. I could see them now, all shapes and sizes, clustered thickly around his desk: His interviews were running ten minutes instead of three; he'd be there till midnight, hungry and frail and tired out. All the same he refused my coffee; all the teachers knew about it and brought their own in thermos flasks.

When I returned to the kitchen, I found Broadside Williams there. He had his arms around Sophie, fooling about and butting her in the chest with his greasy hairdo. He pointed to the marks on her neck and asked us what we thought they were. We all looked away, embarrassed for Sophie.

"They're love bites," said Broadside Williams proudly. He proceeded to give us a demonstration of how you make them. It was fairly gross: Oswald Padkin was shaking badly; he'd closed his eyes to shut it all out. He'd forgotten all about his duties with the stopwatch, but it didn't much matter, for Sophie was squirming about in Broadside's grasp, and every time she squirmed, the bell rang, and the hubbub outside was like the doors opening on a Sears stocktaking clearance.

Then King Arthur burst through the door, red as a rocket fired from a sinking ship. We all shrank back against the wall, except for Broadside, who calmly stood his ground. He released his hold on Sophie and smiled at King Arthur, politely complimenting him on his jacket. It was nice, said Broadside, to see a man these days who took a serious interest in his appearance, particularly if that man was employed by the Education Department. He could tell at a glance, he added, that the jacket had come from George's. And here he actually put his hand out, and patted the stuff of the jacket. "You can feel the quality," he said.

The effect of all this on King Arthur was very strange.

He'd entered the kitchen at high speed, and when he'd seen Broadside there, he'd shot his arm out in a manner that suggested he'd have him by the throat. But now his arm fell down by his side harmlessly, and he stared at Broadside's brawny hand on his lapel in a vacant, wondering fashion. He drew back slightly and gave a little embarrassed cough.

"Well, thank you, Gerald," he said, straightening his tie. "It's nice to meet a boy who has—" He ran his hand through his hair, struggling for a suitable, or even possible, word.

He needn't have taken the trouble; he was talking to thin air. Broadside had slipped out through the door. And at once King Arthur's face went red again, and he turned his wrath on to the rest of us. He wanted to know what the hell we thought we were doing in here: The water in the coffee hadn't been brought to a boil.

James took the lid off the urn and showed him the bubbles. "It's just the generic coffee," he explained. "It tastes like that."

King Arthur raised his meaty hand, then slapped it down helplessly on the sink. Corporal punishment isn't allowed in our school. "If you had to run an institution on the pittance handed out by the Education Department, you'd buy generic too," he cried. He glared at poor Kelly Krake, one of the thin girls who thought she was fat, and told her sharply not to eat the cookies, then turned on Oswald and ordered him to pick up the stopwatch and pull himself together. Finally he shouted at Sophie to get the bell ringing again, every three minutes, no more, no less. He peered at her neck. "You've got a nasty case of ringworm there," he said. His gaze shifted thoughtfully down toward her stomach. "You'd better go to the school nurse on Monday morning," he added.

Sophie started to cry.

"About the ringworm, I mean," he said hastily, backing out the door.

10 THE BAYEUX TAPESTRY was pinned up on the wall; it was the kind of effort most teachers would have kept well out of sight, but Mossy Crocket wasn't like that. She had no instincts of self-preservation; she felt that any kind of art, no matter how bad, should be exhibited. Parents of children whose names did not appear upon the thing were examining it closely and smiling to themselves.

Mrs. Capsella walked all along its length, searching for my piece, or rather, hers. When she found it, she removed the thumbtack and turned the edge of the paper back to see what mark she'd received. It didn't please her; it was, I knew, a D. She took lots of other tacks out and examined other peoples' marks, something that just isn't done, and from the expression on her face I could see that she considered her own mark unjust. I hoped she wouldn't go to Mossy Crocket and complain. Lots of parents did their kids' homework, but none of them would have dared to complain about their marks. I watched with considerable apprehension as she began to walk across the hall in the direction of Mossy's table.

But her attention was distracted by Ms. Rock's family. Ms. Rock's husband was a night worker of some kind, so she'd had to bring all her kids along: There was a little girl of about six sitting on a bench beside the wall, and a baby lying in a basket by her feet. Mrs. Capsella sidled up close and peered in at the baby, which was fast asleep. With its rosy cheeks, long lashes, and a frilly bonnet, it looked rather sweet, but Mrs. Capsella shook her head over it, and I could see her lips silently forming the word "Yuck." She sat down on the bench beside the little girl.

"Is that your sister?" she asked.

The little girl agreed that it was. "There's no sweeter sight in the world than Amy sleeping," she said. You could see that she was the kind of little kid they always pick for TV shows like Romper Room, the kind of kid who isn't ever going to come out with anything gross, who'll always say she loves her mommy and daddy and that her dog's name is Rover. There's no harm in that kind of thing; kids grow out of it.

But Mrs. Capsella was shocked. "Do you really think so?" she asked. She lowered her voice. "Or did someone tell you to say that?"

"I really think so," said the little kid.

Mrs. Capsella shook her head. "You should never think that you think things that you don't think," she said.

I sidled up casually and tried to divert her attention. After all, this was the time of the evening she liked most. By now the teachers were tired and desperate and ready to rat on one another. And there were some teachers who hadn't had many customers at all: They taught subjects like music and needlework and drama, subjects in which the parents had no interest because they wouldn't help their kids to get into college. These teachers always turned up on Parent-Teacher Night. They had nothing much to fear; they brought their knitting and their library books, they appeared relaxed and at ease, but I knew they felt sorry for themselves because no one considered their subjects important. They gazed sullenly across at the teachers who taught math and science; and these teachers, harried and strained and tired, stared back with equal resentment.

I suggested to Mrs. Capsella that she might go and talk to a few of these cases of parental neglect. I didn't take any of their subjects, so they might be surprised to see her; on the other hand it was better than having her undermining Ms. Rock's carefully brought-up child. Already the little girl had abandoned her post by the baby basket and was whispering in her mother's ear. The whisper was quite a loud one for so small a child, and I distinctly heard the words "naughty lady."

"I was just talking to that little girl over there," Mrs. Capsella told me. "It was very interesting: a case of complete—"

"Why don't you go and talk to Miss Purley?" I suggested. "She's hardly had a single parent all night. They don't think music is important."

"Really?" said Mrs. Capsella. "What a shocking thing." She went on, "I had a dream about Miss Purley last night. She was lodging in our house, in the front room, where you kids have those sleep-ins. You know how quiet she is? And how, um, plump? Well, in the dream she was very thin and terribly noisy; you could hear her all over the house, and I couldn't get her to shut up. Every time I spoke to her about the noise, she just laughed in a racketty kind of way." She paused. "It was rather horrible."

The hall was emptying now; it was quieter, and Mrs. Capsella's voice rang out clearly. Several parents looked around.

"You should write a story about it," I said repressively. She winced; any mention of her dubious profession has the effect of silencing her. She got up huffily and made her way to Miss Purley's table.

Ms. Rock's little girl came back, and I offered her some cookies. "I'm not allowed," she said. Then she looked nervously across the room toward Mrs. Capsella. "And I *really* don't like them," she added. "They're yucky."

It was all over at last.

Mr. Capsella was gloomy after his interviews. It was sad really: He'd lost his feeling for the beautiful evening; you couldn't imagine him making remarks about Paradise now. He walked very quietly, his footsteps making no sound on the pavement; he might have been a ghost. I walked rather quietly myself, keeping out of sight. I resolved that from now on, if any teacher blamed me for talking in class when I wasn't, I'd argue with him instead of keeping quiet. I had to clear my name.

All the same, I felt that Mr. Capsella was taking things a bit too seriously. No one had actually complained about my marks, except to say they might be better. The trouble with Mr. Capsella was that he wanted a genius type like Oswald Padkin. He didn't realize that Oswald Padkin, in his own way, would be an equally bad investment too— Mr. Capsella would be spending half his salary on psychiatrists' fees.

As he slouched along sulking, Mrs. Capsella was trying

to cheer him up; I thought she was going the wrong way about it, prancing along by his side, flapping at the snowflake pattern on his sweater with a sheet of paper she'd picked up somewhere.

"Did you get your syllabus?" she asked cruelly.

He didn't answer.

Mrs. Capsella waved the paper under his nose. "The Algebra syllabus!" she cried triumphantly. "The music teacher gave it to me. She used to be married to Mr. Tweedie."

11 N<small>OT SO LONG AGO</small>, in search of a cricket ball beneath the Capsellas' bed, I found a book instead. This discovery gave me a terrific fright: the kind you get when you bite a stone in the brown rice and lose a filling, or see a newspaper headline with W<small>AR</small> in it, even though when you buy the paper and read the story, you find out that the war is only about gasoline prices. You feel as if the earth has stopped moving, just for a second, like in *The Day the Earth Stood Still*, and that when it gets going again, it won't be the same world at all.

It was a pretty commonplace event to find a book under the Capsellas' bed; but this particular one was called *Bringing Up Baby*. Knowing how Mrs. Capsella feels about babies, I couldn't imagine that she'd read a book like this for her own amusement, or to send herself to sleep after a bad day with Madeleine and Imogen and Raoul. It flashed on me that I might be going to have what the Human Relations teacher cutely calls a sibling: that is, a brother or sister.

I stood stock-still in the bedroom, the book clutched damply in my hand, and reviewed the situation. To have an older sibling wouldn't be so bad; both Louis and James had older brothers. They're good for occasional gifts of money and teaching you how to drive, and you can even borrow their clothes, if they have any taste. But mine wouldn't be older, that was pretty obvious, and I knew from friends' experiences that kid brothers and sisters were to be avoided.

There was a time, long ago now, when I'd really wanted a brother or sister like everyone else, but the Capsellas hadn't seemed all that interested. I'd wanted a dog as well, and they hadn't been crazy about that either: Mr. Capsella is nervous with animals. And now, when it was too late, when everyone else's siblings were kids in seventh and eighth grades, it would be just like the Capsellas to produce one.

When all the other mothers were walking around Blaxland Place on their own, window shopping or buying elegant clothes for the older woman, flitting off to fashion shows and art galleries, taking up pottery or even getting respectable jobs, Mrs. Capsella would be hanging around playgrounds and kindergartens with a yowly, red-faced baby bobbing on her chest in one of those hippy slings. The house would smell of talcum powder and diaper soaker, and I wouldn't be able to have my friends over at night. And when little old ladies stopped the new mother in the street to say, "What a lovely little baby," Mrs. Capsella would tell them how, when she was three and a half years old, she had been badly bitten by an infant called Raymond Scoon and had disliked babies ever since. The little old ladies would draw back in horror; they'd look more closely at the baby to see if there were bruises. Or—it was just possible—Mrs. Capsella might turn into one of those mothers you see on television and sometimes in real life, the ones with earnest, eager expressions, who are always talking about bonding and the importance of the father's role.

Anything was possible at Mrs. Capsella's age. I shuddered. I couldn't face these changes: I was too old to have a sibling. I flopped down on the bed with the book still clutched in my hand. I took several deep, calming breaths and forced myself to examine the volume more closely. There was, naturally enough, a baby pictured on the front cover. It was a rosy baby with a bare, fleshy chest and a very white, fleecy diaper; it sat bolt upright on a blue rug, a rattle clutched in one chubby fist. I pondered a little; the chubbiness suggested gross overfeeding, and I knew from my occasional reading of the *Women's Weekly* that overfeeding wasn't in fashion these days. The hairstyle was out of date too, brushed up in the front like a rooster's comb, and the rattle, a garishly colored celluloid cylinder, was the kind you see on television consumer programs, where the lady investigator, with a destructive smile on her lips, pulls the thing apart, pours the lead pellets into the palm of her hand and holds them out for a close-up. "Death trap," she says, shaking her head in a satisfied way.

So the book was out of date—it was old. But that wasn't really a cause for hope—the Capsellas were always prowling around secondhand bookshops; they'd buy anything with print in it. What really cheered me up was the amount of dust on the cover, more dust than you could get in a few weeks, or even months. It was the dust of years. Fourteen, to be exact. It was *my* baby book; inside was a card from Mrs. Capsella's parents, Pearly and Neddy Blount: THERE'S NOTHING LIKE A BABY BOY! it said.

The world slid back into place, with nothing new or nasty in it. I thumbed through the volume, curious to see what kind of principles lay behind my upbringing.

It was pretty obvious that Mrs. Capsella hadn't read much past page one; either that or she'd found the contents such bullshit that she'd thrown it under the bed and forgotten all about it. The first three chapters were all about Routine and how important this was in the Bringing Up of Baby, in the formation of a happy, stable individual. Children, said the author, a Dr. Mervyn Tetch, felt threatened by disorder and became insecure; they liked to have their days all safe and sure and exactly the same, with regular meals and baths, and bedtime always at the same hour.

I knew my baby days hadn't been like this; I could clearly remember eating breakfast food in my high chair in the kitchen, with the sun shining in a square on the left-and wall opposite the window, where the sun only shone at two o'clock on a summer afternoon. A time when, according to Dr. Mervyn Tetch, babies should not only have had their breakfast, but their bath and morning nap and lunch and half their afternoon nap as well.

And I could also remember, equally clearly, watching a horror movie on television about a boy who trained rats to eat people and himself got eaten instead; it was the kind of movie they show only after midnight. I knew I was a baby when I saw it, because I can recall kicking my foot up in alarm and terror every time the rat leader came onto the screen, and there was a close-up of his small red eyes and twitching pointed nose. The foot I kicked had a knitted bootee on it.

I suppose I got fed and washed and put to bed, but I'm sure, familiar as I am with the Capsellas' domestic shiftlessness, that these events would never have taken place at set times. It was no wonder that I'd turned out to be a nervous sort of person, bothered by sleeping problems and taps dripping and clocks ticking and a fear of not being quite normal. I'd needed a firm routine and I hadn't had one.

12 I FOUND MYSELF thinking about routine again when Mrs. Capsella and I set out on a summer visit to her parents, the Blounts. Mr. Capsella wasn't accompanying us. He had a conference in Tasmania. Besides, I knew he was a bit scared of the Blounts, though they were a normal sort of couple. Before his retirement, Neddy had been a factory supervisor, and Pearly was one of Casper Cooley's True Women: She stayed home and cleaned the house and knitted and waited at the window for people to come home.

I hadn't seen them for a while, not since I was a kid of twelve, and though this wasn't all that long ago, I found I could only remember two things about that visit: the cricket match I'd watched on television in their living room, and the fact that everything had always been on time. Meals and baths and the hours when you watched television were fixed: It was rather like staying in a well-ordered, old-fashioned hotel. That was routine, I supposed, though I hadn't known it at the time. Just the kind of thing Dr. Tetch would have approved. And as I sat in a compartment of the Southern Aurora with Mrs. Capsella, watching the weird, treeless Sydney suburbs sliding by the train window, I thought the visit might be pleasant, even good for me, like a rest cure.

Mrs. Capsella didn't seem to be thinking along these lines. She was gazing out at the suburbs in a nervous kind of way, and I noticed that she was biting her nails, something I'd never seen her do before. The nails were painted with a rosy shade of polish. I'd never seen this before either, and it struck me as depressingly typical that the moment she made the effort to improve her rather grubby-looking hands, she'd pick up a habit that ruined the whole effect.

"I don't think we'll stay very long," she muttered, turning from the window. "A couple of days should be enough."

I thought this seemed rather unmannerly; she hadn't seen the Blounts for two years, though it wasn't exactly her fault. They didn't like Communists, whom they called Reds, and they thought Mr. Capsella was one. Mrs. Capsella had explained that he was Labor, but it didn't do any good; the Blounts thought Labor people were the same as Communists. Mrs. Capsella didn't vote for anyone, so she was free to come and go as she wished. She didn't appear to wish to very often. "It doesn't seem very polite to leave so soon," I said.

Mrs. Capsella screwed up her face. When she'd straightened it out, she gazed at me for quite a long time in a way that suggested she felt sorry for me. She made no reply to my remark about politeness.

"Why do we have to leave so soon?" I persisted.

"Well—" She fiddled about with a piece of her hair,

twisting it around her finger and chewing on its soggy end. "There isn't much to do there," she replied limply.

"We can go out," I suggested. "We can go to Bondi Beach." I'd been looking forward to seeing a proper beach, with real waves, instead of the pebbly, shallow kind we have in Melbourne. I'd packed my bathers: Sydney people called bathers "cossies," and they say "carstle" instead of castle, almost like foreigners.

"No, we can't," said Mrs. Capsella flatly. "You were just talking about being polite. It's not polite, when we're visiting, to go out and leave them at home."

"They can come with us."

"No, they can't. They never go out."

"Never?"

"Well, not exactly. They go to the shops, and to the Leagues Club on Saturday nights, but that's about all. They won't go anywhere else."

"Why not?"

"They don't like to. At least Pearly doesn't, and she won't let Neddy go without her. They haven't been into town for thirty years."

Thirty years! More than twice as long as I'd been alive. And the suburb where the Blounts lived was only fifteen miles from the city: from the Harbor and the beaches and all the interesting sights of Kings Cross.

"Is there something the matter with them?" I asked gently.

Mrs. Capsella smiled grimly. "Nothing you could poke a stick at," she replied.

I had a sudden image of Pearly Blount's face, or rather,

her head, and the kind of curlers she wore in her hair. They weren't the colored plastic rollers you see on our neighborhood ladies, when you're walking early to school and catch them bringing in the trash cans and milk bottles: Pearly's curlers were shiny metal, like big butterfly paper clips, with nasty rows of sharp pointy little teeth between their jaws. I wondered now why she bothered to put her hair in curlers if she didn't like to go anywhere.

When we got out of the train at Harris Park and began walking along the little streets toward the Blounts' house, I began remembering other things I'd forgotten. The landscape, for instance: It was so unlike the one I lived in that you might have been on another planet. In our neighborhood all the houses are different styles: big two-storey brick mansions and timber Cape Cod houses with pointed attics; long modern bungalows and ordinary triple-fronted brick veneers. There were different kinds of gardens, too: the old-fashioned kind with neat lawns and flowerbeds, bush gardens and rock gardens and the occasional Capsella-style wilderness. Here in Harris Park everything was exactly the same: all the houses were built in the same style, small cottages in dark-red brick, the front windows shuttered with venetian blinds in washed-out pastel colors. They all had queer, claustrophobic verandas with high brick walls and pillars at each end, red-brick columns with round white stone globes on top. These verandas were so narrow that it was difficult to imagine anyone sitting on them in comfort; there wouldn't have been room to stretch out your legs. And the walls were so high that the sun couldn't have penetrated at all. It would have been dark inside, and cold, like sitting in a well.

The gardens were all the same too: flowerbeds along the fences and beneath the veranda wall, two neat square lawns on either side of a gleaming white front path. The gates had brick pillars like the verandas, with plaster statues perched on top: eagles and lions' heads, even griffins. There was no one around, except for the occasional old gray head stuck between the globes of the verandas. And there wasn't a tree in sight; the whole place was perfectly flat, right to the horizon. That horizon seemed close, because there weren't any trees or hills or even taller buildings, just the narrow streets and telephone poles and the red-brick houses and the sky suddenly coming down at the back of them, so it seemed that if you lived in the last house and walked out your back gate you'd just find empty space. It was rather scary. Mrs. Capsella didn't seem to notice. She was hurrying along, wobbling a little on the high heels she'd changed into back at the Central Station ladies' room. She kept glancing at her watch. "We're a bit late," she said anxiously. "We'll have to hurry, or we won't be in time for tea."

"We had tea on the train."

"I mean dinner," said Mrs. Capsella.

She surprised me. The Capsellas always call the evening meal "dinner" and when I refer to it as "tea" they always correct me. "Dinner, not tea," they cry. Now Mrs. Capsella was saying "tea" herself. I pointed this out to her, and she became cross. "Just say 'tea' while we're here," she snapped. " 'Dinner' sounds snobby."

"I know it does. But when I told you it was posh, you said I'd been picking up—"

"Don't say 'posh'!" screamed Mrs. Capsella. "You know I hate that word."

"It means Port Out, Starboard Home," I informed her.

"What?"

"When the rich English people went out to India on ships, they had the port side out, and the starboard side home, so they'd get the sun, or the shade, I can't remember which."

"That's very interesting," said Mrs. Capsella, slowing down her awkward trot and putting her head on one side, like her old self.

"It's a very clever word," I said. "So I don't see why you hate me using it. And why do I have to say 'tea' at the Blounts' house when you always want me to say 'dinner' at home?"

Mrs. Capsella's momentary pleasantness vanished. "Just be quiet, will you?" she snapped. I was worried. First of all there was the scary landscape, like something in a B-grade horror film; now there was Mrs. Capsella having an attack of split personality. As we hurried along the streets, dragging our overnight bags behind us, turning corner after corner and finding each new street exactly like the one before, she began telling me over and over how to behave at the Blounts' place. I was to put my clothes away neatly and never toss them on the floor; I had to shut the bathroom door when I went in there, to eat all my food, and not to complain about the cooking; and I was on no account to interrupt when Pearly Blount was talking.

She repeated all these instructions several times. I recalled reading about this technique in Dr. Mervyn Tetch's book: You had to repeat each instruction several times to a child, using a firm, level voice, so the kid got the message and felt secure. It was a bit like a manual I'd read years ago, on the training of German shepherds. But Mrs. Capsella's repetitions didn't make me feel secure at all, just plain irritated, and I began to wonder if Dr. Tetch had ever had children of his own, and how they'd turned out. I found I could imagine his offspring quite easily: They'd be dorks, the nasty kind who ran around turning other kids in.

"You don't have to tell me everything sixty times," I complained. "I'm not a baby."

"Sorry," apologized Mrs. Capsella, in her normal voice. She added that her parents were a bit old-fashioned, and she didn't want them to think I was a lout. "Just be careful," she warned. "Only speak when you are spoken to, and if they say anything that sounds odd, don't say, 'That's bullshit.'"

"How do you mean, 'odd'?"

"Oh, never mind," said Mrs. Capsella. "Let's not talk about it. I've got a headache."

13 WE ARRIVED at the Blounts' house. It was the same red brick as all the others, with the same pillared veranda, but it stood out because it was even neater than all the other neat houses. The grass was so flat and green, it seemed artificial; you felt it might be possible to roll the whole thing up like a mat. The bushes were clipped back tight; they seemed to cower—you suspected they wouldn't dare to lose a leaf. There was a single pink rose on a bush beneath the veranda; it was curled up fast and small, and somehow I felt sure it wouldn't get past that stage. The path between the gate and the veranda was so dazzling white, it might have been taken off a clothesline five minutes ago. On the brick pillars beside the gate sat two big plaster labradors.

Neddy Blount was in the garden, doing something to a frangipani bush beside the fence. He was picking off flowers and laying them neatly in a cardboard grocery box beside his feet. All the time we were exchanging greetings, I couldn't take my eyes off his feet; they were very long and narrow, and you noticed them particularly because Neddy was such a small man, no more than five feet tall. And he wore striking, white-canvas shoes—not sneakers or track shoes or docksiders, but the old-fashioned kind you see hanging in the dusty windows of little seaside stores. Sand shoes. They were as dazzling as the path. Neddy caught me staring at them and seemed pleased by my attention.

"Dunlop," he said, and added that it was difficult to find a decent pair of sand shoes these days, with all the fancy foreign trash they had in the shops. "How old would you say these are?" he asked.

For some extraordinary reason this simple query made me blush. I was convinced I was going to give the wrong answer and that my mistake would make me look modern, or foreign, or even Communist, like Mr. Capsella. But I couldn't stay silent, because Neddy was waiting for my answer, his bright blue eyes shining expectantly, like a friendly dog who waits for you to throw him a stick.

"Um—three months," I said. They couldn't be much older than that—the laces hadn't gone stringy.

"Five years!" cried Neddy triumphantly. "Bought them at Slasher's Discount Store, in October, the Wednesday after Labor Day five years ago. Seven dollars—three pounds ten in the Good Old Currency." He went on to say that there was nothing like the local product—provided you took care of it properly. He proceeded to give me a detailed account of the care involved: He scrubbed them down each night with an old nailbrush and something called Good Old Sunlight. Then he applied a good solid coat of Kiwi White, the kind that came in cans, not the fancy gimmicky contraptions with bits of sponge in the top. You got a lot of people these days, he said, who wasted good money on gadgets like that, people who didn't know any better, college types and New Australians.

"What are New Australians?" I asked.

"Well—" began Neddy. He beamed at me, pleased with the question; he was a man who liked to give explanations. But there was a tinge of surprise in his tone, as if he thought it strange I didn't know. He took a deep breath, "Well—you've got your dagos, and then there's your—"

Mrs. Capsella interrupted. "What are you doing with the frangipani bush?" she asked.

Neddy seemed equally pleased with this question, though a bit dazed at having so many explanations to give at once. Mrs. Capsella seemed eager to have her question answered first. This surprised me; her interest in gardening could only be described as minimal. "Why are you taking the flowers off?" she persisted.

Neddy smiled indulgently at his daughter. "Not *all* the flowers, Ellen," he said. "Only the ones that are a bit brown around the edges. Otherwise they fall off by themselves and clutter up the lawn. You wouldn't believe the mess it makes—there's a place across the road where they leave them there to *rot*. Number twenty-three, just over there." He looked at me. "Did you see it as you came past?"

"I don't think so," I replied.

"Come on—I'll show you." Neddy padded across the lawn toward the gate, beckoning us to follow. We left our bags on the path (they looked quite untidy there) and trailed after him out of the gate and across the road. We couldn't really do anything else, though it seemed odd to go off again when we'd only just arrived. We did try staying on the lawn for a moment, but Neddy kept on calling us, standing in the middle of the road and waving his arms like a policeman. Soon all three of us were standing in a little cluster outside the front gate of number twenty-three while Neddy pointed out the mess beneath their frangipani bush. "Fifteen minutes a day," he muttered. "That's all it takes." He shook his head sadly. "Too busy watching videos."

A face appeared at the front window, and the curtains twitched angrily. "Let's go," urged Mrs. Capsella, but Neddy lingered, leaning over the low brick wall to point out an old potato-chip packet wedged by the side of a bush. "Been there since Tuesday last," he said.

Mrs. Capsella pulled at his arm. "Come *on*," she cried. "Mum is probably waiting for us."

Something like alarm passed over Neddy's mild, horsey face. "Right," he said. "Okey-doke." But as we crossed over to our own side of the street, he kept turning his head to look back at number twenty-three. "You've got to keep an eye on people like that," he told us.

As we climbed the steps to the veranda, we saw that Pearly Blount was indeed waiting for us, standing behind the screen of the security door. It was a very dark screen, crisscrossed with a heavy steel lattice; you could see out but not in. All the same, you knew Pearly was there, because you could make out the pale glow of one of the pink sweaters she always wore; she made them herself and called them "woollies." You could also hear her voice.

"Well, well, well," she was saying. "Hullo, strangers." I didn't much like the way she said that; it sounded as if we'd done something wrong. There was a jingling as she twisted the key in the lock; I must say it seemed strange to me that the door was locked at all, with Neddy just outside in the garden. She held the door open about a foot with her tiny little wrinkly hand. She wore red nail polish, a brighter, darker shade than Mrs. Capsella's. I stepped forward.

"There's a mat there," said Pearly.

I'd noticed the mat, a large, square, brown doormat with WELCOME printed on it in big black letters. You could tell from the sharpness of those letters, so black the ink looked wet, that the mat was very new, or else no one used it much. Perhaps it was new, and Pearly was proud of it. I remembered Mrs. Capsella's advice about being polite, and I said pleasantly, "It's a very nice mat."

Pearly didn't reply to this compliment, and she didn't open the door any wider. "It's a doormat," she hissed.

"I know."

"She means you're supposed to wipe your feet on it," prompted Mrs. Capsella.

" 'She' is the cat's mother," said Pearly Blount.

I wiped my feet and the door was opened, and then swiftly closed again, just as Neddy came up the steps onto the veranda.

"*Not* in your garden clothes!" exclaimed Pearly. "What on earth are you thinking of?"

Neddy stepped back, grinning rather sheepishly. "Right!" he said. "Okey-doke." He disappeared back down the steps and ambled off around the side of the house.

"In his *garden* clothes!" Pearly repeated in tones of amazement. "He's never done that before!" She stared repressively at Mrs. Capsella and me, as if we were somehow to blame. "Well!" she said again.

I felt very tall in that house. When I'm with my friends, I feel smallish, because, apart from Louis, they're all so much bigger. But Mrs. Capsella and her parents were tiny people, and I was the odd man out. Pearly was only four six. If she'd been born in the modern age, she might have made a career for herself as a female jockey. The Blounts went in for chandeliers, and they had them hung low. Before I'd been inside the house ten minutes, I'd knocked my head on two of them, like a clownish character in a silent movie.

"Tall, isn't he?" remarked Pearly, as if there was something wrong with that.

"The poor fellow can't help it," said Neddy kindly. He'd changed his clothes somewhere out back, and Pearly had let him inside. Tea was ready on the table and we all sat down to eat.

"Bertie's just made that way," continued Neddy. "Tall."

The Blounts always called me Bertie; they thought my real name was Albert; the Capsellas didn't seem to have told them about Almeric. I rather liked Bertie; I regretted that I hadn't thought of it myself, years back. It was too late now; I was stuck with Al.

Neddy put his head on one side like Mrs. Capsella and regarded me with his bright eyes. "He's like poor old Blackie," he said.

Poor old Blackie wasn't a dog, it seemed, but a man with black hair, an old friend of Neddy's, who had died of a heart attack the year before.

"Want to know what he *really* died of?" asked Neddy.

Once again I didn't know quite what to say. Mrs. Capsella's repetitive warnings about behavior had made me uncertain. It seemed rather prying to say yes—being curious about how people died seemed in poor taste, but then so did calling black-haired people "Blackie." But if I said I wasn't interested in the real cause of his death, then I might sound rude. I puzzled a bit, and then I remembered Mrs. Capsella saying, "Just speak when you're spoken to." I was being spoken to. "Mmm," I said. It could be interpreted as either yes or no.

"Not smoking," said Neddy triumphantly, jabbing me in the ribs.

The answer really shook me. What did it mean? Plenty of people died of smoking, but how could you die of not smoking? "How could you die of not smoking?" I said aloud.

Neddy seemed pleased with my question, just as he'd been pleased with the one about New Australians. He told me that Blackie Mulligan had his heart attack because he was always rushing about, he'd been like that all his life, he'd never taken a moment off to sit down and relax.

"When you smoke," he said, "you've got to sit down, right?"

"Well—right."

"Okey-doke. *Now*—" he reached into his pocket and took out a piece of paper, then unclipped one of the pens he wore fastened to his shirt. "The average cigarette takes six minutes to smoke—right?"

"I guess so."

"It does. And say you're an average smoker, a pack a day, that's twenty-five. Six times twenty-five?"

"One hundred and fifty."

"Right. That's two and a half hours a solid day relaxation. And say you smoke for fifty years. That's two and a half times three hundred and sixty-five, um—" He scribbled rapidly on his piece of paper. "That's nine hundred and twelve hours a year or thereabouts—times fifty—"

It was all beyond me, and not just the mathematics.

"That's forty-five thousand six hundred hours of solid relaxation! See what I mean? Poor old Blackie. If he'd only seen the light, if he'd only *smoked*, he'd be here today."

"But smoking makes you tense."

"What?"

"It makes you tense; it increases your blood pressure and puts a strain on your heart. Even if you're sitting down. If your friend had smoked, he would have died sooner."

There was a thick silence about the tea table. I was a little sorry I'd spoken; it was pretty obvious from their yellow fingers and the yellow curtains hanging at the window, as well as the pall of smoke about the house, that the Blounts were heavy smokers. They were old, too. And then, I didn't really like throwing a spoke into the wheels of Neddy's theories; he seemed so delighted with them. It was sad to see the delight fade out in his face and give way to bewilderment. He sat chewing at the end of his pen, mulling over these new, mean facts. Then he brightened again. He banged his fist on the edge of the table and said airily, "Oh, that's all doctors' rubbish. You don't want to listen to that killjoy rubbish, Bertie. Ratbaggery."

"But—" I began. Then I felt a sharp kick on my ankle from Mrs. Capsella's side of the table.

Pearly Blount was staring disapprovingly into my face, her lips bunched up together, the top one furrowed with a fan of tiny little pleats—she'd got that from smoking. "He's got a big mouth," she remarked to Mrs. Capsella.

"Oh, I wouldn't say that, Pearly," said Neddy mildly. "It's not Bertie's fault. They teach them lots of fancy things at the schools these days."

"They teach them to have big mouths," said Pearly stubbornly. She turned her attention to Mrs. Capsella, who was shifting the food about her plate with nervous hands. "Eat your food before it gets cold," Pearly told her sharply.

Pearly was a good cook: Her meals looked just like the ones in the margarine advertisements; nothing was raw or charred, and all the vegetables were neatly separated and arranged clockwise around the plate. The only problem was that she'd given me peas. I've never been able to eat peas of any kind, fresh or frozen or canned; they make me feel sick. Mrs. Capsella never gave me peas. I knew that Pearly was going to notice I'd left them; she had the sharpest eyes I'd ever seen, and she always seemed to be waiting for people to do something wrong, just as Neddy was always waiting for them to ask questions so he could reel out the answers. Now she waited until all the plates were quite, quite empty (except for my peas) and all the knives and forks laid down beside them. Then she pounced.

"What about your peas?"

"I don't eat peas," I said, and of course she wanted to know why not.

"I don't like them," I said faintly. It somehow seemed less rude than saying that they made me sick.

"Like! What about all the starving little girls and boys in China?"

"India, Pearly," said Neddy. "The Reds have plenty of food these days with all that forced labor. Plenty of peas."

"In India, then," said Pearly, darting him a cross look.

Again I couldn't think what to say. I had a feeling that if you lived in the Blounts' house for long enough, you'd stop talking altogether. Mrs. Capsella, who was generally quite noisy, had hardly said a word all evening.

"Peas make your hair curly," said Pearly.

I couldn't think of anything worse than having curly hair, but I didn't say so. Pearly had curls herself, from the sharp-toothed curlers. Neddy rejoined the conversation, telling us all that he'd eaten peas for seventy-three years and never regretted it for an instant. He recited a poem I remembered from kindergarten:

> *"I eat my peas with honey—*
> *I've done it all my life.*
> *They do taste kind of funny,*
> *But it keeps them on my knife."*

He asked me if he could pass me the honey.

"Don't make a joke of it, Neddy," said Pearly sternly. She leaned across the table toward me. "When I was a little girl," she said, "and I wouldn't eat my porridge for breakfast, do you know what my father did?"

I shook my head. It was difficult to imagine Pearly having a father, somehow.

"Well," she began, "first he used to say, 'Leave the table.' Then he'd get my mother to put the porridge in the ice chest, and at dinnertime that porridge would be back on the table, and there again at tea time; it would come back at every single meal, and I wouldn't get a bite of anything else until I'd eaten every single scrap of it." As she spoke, Pearly's sharp little eyes grew larger and larger and lost their glitter; they misted over like tiny wind-shields, and her voice collapsed in a croak. She gulped, and her cheeks wobbled. I felt sorry for her. My great-grandfather sounded like a monster.

"Gee," I said sympathetically, "he must have been off."

"Off?" enquired Neddy, interest gleaming in his eyes. "What does 'off' mean?"

"Well—you know—crazy."

"Crazy?" repeated Pearly.

"Insane, then."

Pearly Blount turned bright red. "I'll have you know my father was a perfectly normal man," she said.

"Just strict," said Neddy. "That's all."

"He had a heart of gold," sniffed Pearly. "Pure gold."

"Al is allergic to peas, Mum," said the silent Mrs. Capsella. "I meant to tell you."

"It's not normal to be allergic to things," cried Pearly. "You should have him seen to."

After tea Neddy Blount took a key ring from his pocket and went toward the windows. He inserted a small key into a little lock at the side of the frame and slid the window back. Then he moved to the next one.

"Know what I'm doing?" he asked me.

"Opening the windows."

"Right. The house is air-conditioned, so we keep the windows closed. It gets a bit musty, so every evening I open them, at five fifteen, just to get a breath of fresh air. Then I close them at five twenty-five. I do the same in the mornings; open at six forty-five, closed at six fifty-five. Right?"

"Right."

"Okey-doke." He went through the door, rattling his keys like a jailer happy in his work. I followed in his footsteps and watched the windows sliding open all over the house. There wasn't much else to do.

As I passed the door of Mrs. Capsella's room, I saw her standing inside. She beckoned me in. "I need some air," she hissed.

"Neddy's just opening the windows."

"For heaven's sake! I mean I need to get *out* in the air. I'm going for a walk."

"I'll come," I whispered. "Don't leave me behind."

We walked quietly up the hall toward the front door.

"Where are you going?" called Pearly from the living room.

It was a little after five thirty. Bathed already, clad in a rosy-pink dressing gown, she was sitting in a big black armchair in front of the television. There was a little table beside the chair with all her things on it: glasses case and knitting book and two balls of pink wool, her cigarettes and lighter and a big jar of Arctic mints. She always sucked mints when she smoked; she said she couldn't stand the taste of tobacco. Neddy sat close by in a big brown armchair, nodding a bit, as if he wasn't very fond of television.

"We're just going for a walk," said Mrs. Capsella.

"Walk?" echoed Pearly. Do you mean you're going *outside*?"

Neddy, jerked awake, seemed surprised as well. He said he always took his walk in the mornings, at nine fifteen.

"I have to get a stamp," said Mrs. Capsella, waving a rather tacky-looking envelope she'd taken from her pocket.

"We have stamps in the house," said Pearly. "Dad will get you one." She nudged Neddy, and blinking a little, he hauled himself out of the chair and padded over to the sideboard. "Here you are," he said, holding out a stamp.

"Thanks," said Mrs. Capsella guiltily, keeping the letter hidden behind her back so Pearly wouldn't notice that it was an old electricity bill. She backed off down the hall again, rather quickly and on tiptoe.

"Where are you going now?" called Pearly.

"To the mailbox."

"The last post has gone," said Pearly. "It goes at five. You've missed it." She told Mrs. Capsella to give the letter to Neddy; he'd post it in the morning when he went on his walk.

Mrs. Capsella kept on walking toward the door. "I need the exercise," she said. "I'm thirty-nine and I don't smoke; I might have a heart attack."

Pearly got up from her chair and followed us up the hall; so did Neddy. As we walked down the garden path and past the labradors guarding the gate, the Blounts stood on the veranda steps, watching us with bewildered eyes. I felt mean, but couldn't figure out why.

We walked a long way through the streets of red-brick houses, crossing a railway line and a plot of waste ground. Beyond these the landscape changed suddenly. It was still flat, and the houses all the same as one another, but they were poorer houses, small, shabby prefab ones with their paint all washed away, their scraggy yards full of dust and weeds and rusting pieces of iron. I was nervous; it looked the kind of place where you might find hoods hanging around, the kind of place you could get bashed up. Mrs.

Capsella didn't seem unnerved at all, which surprised me. At home, where it wasn't really necessary, she never stopped worrying about muggers and child molesters. Here, in a sinister neighborhood where it seemed to me a person might well disappear without a trace, she didn't turn a hair.

Sure enough, in the yard of a house across the street, I saw a gang of hoods in tight jeans and long checked shirts, fooling around with a big fancy car, a vintage model, complete with brass headlights and running board. I felt sure they'd ripped it off: For one thing, they were taking off the license plates.

Instead of hurrying by, Mrs. Capsella actually crossed the road and advanced towards the group. "Hi," she said.

The hoods were surprised as hell; she just walked through the gate and stood among them in a friendly way. She asked the biggest hood how his mother was. He seemed embarrassed, and fiddled with his hair. "Fine," he muttered.

"Nice car!" exclaimed Mrs. Capsella. "My uncle Pat had one just like it." She climbed on the running board and peered through the windows. "Lovely dashboard, isn't it?"

The hoods muttered to each other. I pulled Mrs. Capsella away with some difficulty and hurried her on up the street. She kept turning back to wave.

"That was Raymond Scoon," she said in a pleased voice. "I used to play marbles with him."

Marbles! As if hoods play marbles!

I said, "It can't be anyone you used to play marbles with; they were all too young."

"Raymond Scoon was younger than me—about four

years younger. He was that baby I told you about, the one that bit me."

"Listen, Mum—if he was four years younger than you, he'd be thirty-five now. That yob was only about eighteen."

"Don't say 'yob,' or I'll put you in another school."

"All right. But that *boy* wasn't anywhere near thirty-five, so he's not Raymond Scoon."

She frowned. "But he was in Raymond Scoon's house, and he looked just like him."

"Probably his son."

"His *son!*" she exclaimed, then sighed. "Time flies," she said.

She seemed thoughtful, even depressed, as we turned and began walking back in the direction of the Blounts' house. As we crossed the last street before the block of wasteland, a huge black car screeched around the corner, missing us by inches. As it roared by, horns blaring, I caught a glimpse of Raymond Scoon Jr.'s evil face at the window. I clutched at Mrs. Capsella. "They're trying to run us down," I cried. "Get a move on, will you!"

"Who? What are you talking about?"

"Scoon and his mates—they probably think we're going to the cops about that vintage car. They ripped it off, you know."

"Rubbish," said Mrs. Capsella irritably. "What a little snob you are. This always was a dangerous corner."

As we crossed the railway tracks, she glanced uneasily behind her—but it wasn't the hoods she was worried about. "Don't tell Mum where we've been," she said. "She never knew I played around here."

14 OVER THE NEXT FEW DAYS I became accustomed to the Blounts' routines, from the first squeak of the windows opening at six forty-five, to the chink of the milk bottles placed on the front steps at five past ten. In between there was breakfast and dinner and tea and morning and afternoon tea, there was Neddy's walk at nine fifteen and Pearly Blount's housework, and the long afternoon when Neddy worked in the garden and Pearly knitted her pink woollies on the claustrophobic veranda, sitting bolt upright so there would be room for her tiny feet in the narrow space.

There wasn't much for us to do. Mrs. Capsella tried helping with the housework, but Pearly said politely that she thought she'd be quicker on her own. She gave Mrs. Capsella a book to keep her occupied; it was called *Nurse in Peril* and might well have been one of Mrs. Capsella's works.

I hung out with Neddy in the garden. I trimmed the lawn edges with a pair of shiny shears and pulled the browning flowers off the frangipani bush while Neddy pruned and clipped the rest of the foliage. We wheeled the clippings around to the back garden, where there was a row of compost heaps like small haystacks lined up beside the garden shed. The grass clippings and flowers went on one heap, the twigs upon another. Everything was very neat and tidy, a little like Dr. Spinner's library: a place for everything and everything in its place.

Neddy asked if I was interested in waste disposal.

"Like the Bag of Mysteries?" I asked. This was Neddy's name for the plastic bag he brought into the kitchen after every meal, when he went carefully around all the plates, collecting chop bones and scraps of fat and storing it all away in the freezer until Wednesday night, when the garbage men came around. He said it stopped the trash cans from smelling.

He smiled now. "This is on a larger scale altogether, Bertie," he said. He explained that the city wouldn't collect garden waste, so he'd figured out a way to get the better of them. He unlocked the door of the garden shed. "Take a look inside," he urged.

The shed was lined with shelves, and the shelves were filled with parcels. Very neat parcels, about the size of shoe boxes, wrapped in newspaper and tied up with string. They looked exciting, as parcels always do before you know what's inside them.

"What are they?" I asked.

"Leaves," replied Neddy. "And twigs. I pop five or six of these parcels in the trash cans every week." He chuckled. "They think it's rubbish."

"But it is."

"*Garden* rubbish," said Neddy. "They think it's proper rubbish."

I glanced around the shelves and made a few calculations. At five or six a week, Neddy would be pushing the double-century mark before he got rid of this lot. I wondered if Mrs. Capsella would inherit.

We spent the rest of the afternoon making up more parcels. The grass and frangipani flowers were easy to manage, but the twigs presented problems; you had to strip the leaves off and break the twigs up into tiny pieces. It seemed a funny way to pass the time; a few days back I might have said abnormal—now I didn't like to. But I found myself wondering if kindly Neddy wasn't just a trifle crazy. It seemed unkind to think so, because he was a pleasant man and happy in his work, but I was a little worried in case madness was hereditary.

I found it terribly hard to get to sleep in the Blount's house, even though from the moment I had first stepped through Pearly's security door, I'd felt really tired. My eyes had grown heavy, like they do when you're catching a cold, and my face felt oddly stiff. Perhaps it was all the cigarette smoke in the air; you could get a pain in the chest from just thinking about it. And I found that living in an orderly household, where everything was done just so and always right on time, didn't have a soothing effect at all. It didn't give me a sense of security; I wasn't reassured, but nervous: I began feeling that if tea wasn't ready exactly at four forty-five, if Neddy didn't open the windows at a quarter to seven in the morning and close them ten minutes later, then something bad would happen. You didn't know what, but you kept on waiting for it. And the neat, clean, quiet rooms had the same queer effect: You felt that they were all prepared for something, waiting, that the furniture, the tables and chairs and the sofa and china cabinet had a second, secret life of their own. Perhaps they came alive at night and walked about and spoke to each other like the toys in *The Magic Toyshop*. I wondered if Dr. Mervyn Tetch's kids had felt like this as they lived their carefully ordered lives; I wondered if they were grown up now and living in lunatic asylums with names like Paradise Gardens and Sunnyside Grange.

It was so quiet there at night. After ten o'clock, when the television was switched off and the milk bottles put out and everyone brushed their teeth in turn (closing the bathroom door) and then went off to bed, there wasn't a sound. You couldn't hear anything except your own breathing, really loud and whistly, like Louis with an asthma attack coming on. Even outside it was quiet: no cars rushing by, no doors banging or neighbors shouting good-bye to visitors, not even a cat fight or a dog barking. It was different at home, where at any time of night you might wake up and hear something going on, Mrs. Capsella scratching away at her desk or Mr. Capsella whining about his students, the bashing of the coffee grinder or the taps being turned on and off.

It had irritated me in the past, the way they rattled about all night and kept waking me up; now I found I didn't like the quiet—it seemed, strangely, abnormal. The word "normal" bothered me now. Pearly Blount used it a lot, and every time she did, I felt faintly embarrassed. After all, it was a word I used rather frequently myself, and I was beginning to think it wasn't a very good one. It didn't seem to mean anything; it was just a word people used to say what *they* liked was right, and what other people liked was wrong. Worrying about being normal was like being in prison, and talking about other people being abnormal was like being a prison guard, keeping other people boxed in.

As I lay in the Blounts' spare room, with all these thoughts milling around in my head, I became conscious of the clock on the sideboard. It was a large, old-fashioned one inside a wooden case. It didn't tick fast and quiet like the clocks at home; it *tocked*, a big, fat, slow tock. It struck the hours and the half hours and the quarters in between with great *bongs*. I hated it. And on the second night I decided to do something about it. First I slid out of bed and went to the window; I felt I needed fresh air for the task ahead. Outside it was bright moonlight and the lawn was green, a dark ghostly green with purple shadows beneath the bushes. Nothing moved at all, as if the whole place were clamped down under glass. I examined the window frame; it was different from the ones in the rest of the house—it was the old wooden kind that goes up and down, and there was no lock. I pushed and it opened protestingly with a rubbery, squeaky sound. A current of air passed over the sill, cool and clammy, but it felt good to me. I knew I'd have to get up early in the morning before Neddy came by on his window rounds and noticed it was open.

Now I turned to the matter of shutting up the clock. This was difficult, because it was the wind-up kind, so you couldn't just take the batteries out. I could have carried it outside or to another room, but I was worried that Neddy or Pearly might get up and find it. The only thing was to muffle it, so I wrapped it carefully in a couple of sweaters, then opened the wardrobe door and shoved it into the farthest corner. The tock was silenced; you could still hear the bong, but faintly, and I felt I'd get used to it.

I closed my eyes and found myself thinking of Broadside Williams. I wondered how he'd act if you set him down inside such an orderly house, with Neddy and Pearly Blount. I wondered if he'd go quiet or if he'd stay his ordinary self. Somehow I just couldn't picture him inside the house at all, and suddenly I knew why. It was because you'd never get him in it; he'd take one look at the Blounts' front gate with the big plaster labradors perched on each side, at the perfect garden and the dazzling white path leading up to the security door, and he'd shout "Shit!" and run straight back to the railway station. He was a survivor.

My eyes were just closing when I heard a faint tap on the door. I was certain it was Mrs. Capsella, that she'd been lying there like me, listening to the clock tocking and bonging and feeling sad without her notebooks and her typewriter and Mr. Capsella's instructive conversation. She might have decided to run away home.

But when I opened the door, Pearly Blount was standing there in her rosy dressing gown and cruel curlers. She seemed smaller than ever, and even rather anxious looking. She walked in, and her eyes sped straight to the empty space on the sideboard where the clock had stood.

"Where's Big Ben?" she asked.

"I put it in the wardrobe," I said guiltily. "I couldn't sleep because it tocked so loud."

"Really?" said Pearly in a tone that could almost be described as sympathetic. Her blue eyes weren't as glinty as usual, and her voice was less sharp, as if, like the furniture, she became human at night. She confided that she sometimes suffered from sleeping problems herself, though this evening she'd gone out like a light. But something had woken her up; she'd lain there listening for ages, then realized what the matter was: She couldn't hear Big Ben. That had worried her; the house didn't seem normal without Big Ben ticking. She'd had to come and find out what had happened; she knew she wouldn't sleep a wink till she did.

I opened the wardrobe door and unwrapped Big Ben. He boomed the quarter: two fifteen. Pearly smiled at the sound. "Perhaps you could put it in your room," I suggested. This idea seemed to disturb her; she put up a hand and fiddled with her curlers. "He's always been here," she said uncertainly, gazing up at the sideboard. He's the Guest Room Clock."

"But you like him," I said. "You could hear him better in your room."

I could see that the idea really appealed to her, and she took Big Ben from me and moved toward the doorway, holding him firmly against her chest. But at the doorway she hesitated, her eyes fixed on the sideboard, a struggling, bewildered expression in her eyes.

"You could put him back again," I suggested. "After we've gone home."

Her face brightened. "Yes, I could, couldn't I?" she said.

So that was that: I lay down and listened to her footsteps padding down the hall, and the door closing softly, and Big Ben tocking faintly through the wall. I counted one more bong before I fell asleep.

15 AT NINE FIFTEEN every morning when Neddy
went off for his daily walk, I accompanied
him. It was the only way of escaping the
house, because Pearly was so funny about
people going out. You were only supposed to go out at the
proper times: Wednesday afternoon for the shopping at
Slasher's Discount Store, and Saturday nights for the
Leagues Club. You weren't supposed to go out in between.
Pearly didn't exactly try to stop you, but if you looked like
you were going out, she'd act so surprised that you began
to think there might be something queer in it after all. She
talked a lot about her elder sister Rowdy, who sometimes
came to stay with the Blounts when she was down from
the country, and who spent her evenings going out to visit
friends. Pearly thought it strange that a grown woman
should want to ride around the streets at night in taxis,
dropping in at other people's houses, when she could have
stayed home and watched television in the Blounts' living
room.

Rowdy had gone out in the afternoons as well and been
late back to tea three times; Pearly said it "put her out"
when people weren't on time for tea. She felt funny, and
her evening was all at sixes and sevens. I wasn't quite sure

what she meant by "put her out," but I guessed it had nothing to do with being out of doors. Pearly hated fresh air. "Rowdy treats the house like a hotel," she sulked.

Mrs. Capsella smiled. "You make her sound like a teenager," she giggled. (Rowdy Finn was eighty-four.)

"That's what I meant," replied Pearly. "It's not normal."

Neddy had five different walking routes, one for each day of the working week. He didn't walk on the weekends. The routes were all pretty much the same: along the rows and rows of red-brick houses with their narrow verandas and neat gardens. Neddy never went near the place where Raymond Scoon lived—perhaps he didn't know it was there. Only the names of the streets showed you were in a different area. Today, Neddy informed me, we were walking in India, because all the streets had Indian names: Bengal Crescent and Simla Road and Chandigarh Avenue. The day before we'd done England: Essex Road and Suffolk Avenue, even Park Lane.

We walked at a pretty slow pace, because Neddy liked to peer through fences and over walls to see how the gardens inside were kept. He also liked to look for dogs. He was fond of dogs; every time he went in and out of his own gate, he paused to pat the labradors. And dogs seemed to like him; they came up to gates and stuck their noses through to sniff his hand, then followed him down the length of their fences, tails wagging joyfully.

At the corner of Simla Road and Madras Street we found a lost dog. At least Neddy said it was lost—I wasn't so sure. It was true that it was unusual in this neighborhood to see a dog out on the street, but this one didn't behave as lost dogs usually do, running along the road in a hurried way, all panicky, raising hopeful eyes when it heard a footstep. It was strolling along in a peaceful, leisurely manner, sniffing along the grass of the nature strips and the bases of the telephone poles. It seemed more like a dog out for a walk, taking the air, enjoying the sun and the smells in the grass.

"It's wearing a collar," I pointed out.

"But there's no tag on it," said Neddy, shaking his head. He reached into the pocket of his beige trousers and pulled out a stout length of rope, which he proceeded to fasten around the dog's collar.

"Are you taking it home?" I asked. An image of Pearly, standing forbiddingly behind the screen of the security door, flashed into my mind. I felt sure the arrival of a dog would "put her out." Neddy might have had the same thought. A faint flicker of alarm showed in his eyes, the same flicker I'd noticed that first evening, when Mrs. Capsella had said, "Mum is probably waiting." "No, no," he sighed. "I don't think we'll do that. Just down to the police station." He added pleasantly, "Dogs are well looked after there."

The police station was a small square house behind the Baptist church, a neat weatherboard, painted gray, with an old-fashioned white-picket fence. It seemed like a miracle after all those red-brick houses. The garden was the kind you see beside some country railway stations, with beds of lavender and thyme and rosemary, and there were ferns in pots hanging from the roof of the veranda—a real veranda, airy and spacious, with a well-swept wooden floor. It seemed peaceful and quiet there; a young policeman was watering the ferns with a green spouted can.

"G'day, Clarrie," said Neddy as we passed.

Inside, an older man in a white shirt and suspenders stood behind a high counter, filling in forms.

"G'day, Jim," said Neddy.

Jim pushed the forms aside. "Bloody paperwork," he said. "Useless as a glass eye at a keyhole." He lifted up the flap on the counter and came through toward us. "Got another one for us, eh, Neddy?" he said when he saw the dog. "Where'd you get this one?"

"Corner of Simla Road and Madras Street."

Jim rubbed his chin thoughtfully. "Had a call from the owners of that blue heeler you brought in last Tuesday. The one you said looked kind of thin. Thirty-one London Court. They couldn't understand how it come to get lost."

"Must have left the gate open," said Neddy, looking down at his shoes. "Want me to take it back? We can go around London Court way."

"No need for that, thanks all the same. Clarrie dropped it back this morning on his rounds."

"Did it go through the gate?" asked Neddy mysteriously.

"Right as rain," said Jim carefully. "No worries there, mate." He bent down and patted the dog on the head, and it whined a bit. Although it had seemed happy enough on the street, it was anxious now, a bit bewildered by its walk through strange places at the end of Neddy's rope and the unfamiliarity of the police station. It seemed like a real lost dog now, panic in its eye, little shivers running through its coat like wind through a wheat field.

"Like to take him round the back, then?" said Jim.

The backyard of the police station was like a little market garden: lettuce and silver beet coming up nicely in the loamy beds, graveled paths in between. Near the back fence was a long, roomy wire cage with a wooden shelter in the back. Several dogs of various shapes and sizes lay stretched out in the sun. They stood up when they spied Neddy and hurried to the gate in a friendly fashion, wagging their tails. The new dog, pushed through the gate, sat in a corner by himself, shyly.

"He'll soon get acclimatized," said Neddy confidently.

"What did you mean—about that other dog—when you asked Jim if he went in the gate all right?" I asked Neddy on the way home.

"It's a test," he replied. "Sure-fire. If they won't go in the owner's gate, if they act nervous, worried, it means they've been ill treated. Then I bring them straight back here. Better safe than sorry."

"Mmm," I said.

As we walked back up Suffolk Avenue, hurrying a little, for we were later than usual and Pearly would be waiting in the window, I began wishing that Neddy had a dog of his own. But I could understand why he didn't; a dog would put Pearly out, and perhaps even Neddy as well. It wouldn't know the ropes and would mess up their orderly routines. A dog wouldn't know it was supposed to wipe its feet on the doormat; it would want meals at odd hours, bark in the night, and treat the place like a hotel. But I thought it might be trained, and I felt that Neddy would like this: I could imagine him drawing up a timetable for the training sessions, and for walks and meals, even building a kennel in the backyard, behind the row of little haystacks.

Pearly was the real problem; she'd say that having a dog wasn't normal for a man of Neddy's age. A dog would be new and difficult in the house, and she didn't like anything that was unfamiliar: This was what she really meant when she sniffed and said, "It's not normal." It was almost a kind of fear.

And it also had something to do with belonging; it was always other people's possessions or ways that were queer, or abnormal. It never occurred to her for a moment that anything that was her own, like the cruel hair curlers or the pink woollies or not being able to sleep at night unless she could hear Big Ben ticking, might seem queer to other people. This gave me an idea.

On the last morning of our visit we went out to buy presents for Neddy and Pearly. Mrs. Capsella said she was fed up with thinking of excuses to get out of the house; we'd just go, and say nothing. So when Pearly Blount was locked up in the bathroom and Neddy was in the shed with his parcels, we slipped out and ran all the way down the street to the first corner. Once around it we felt safe and began to walk at an ordinary pace, enjoying the sun and the fresh air. But I found I kept on thinking of Pearly coming out of the bathroom and finding we weren't in the house; I imagined her walking through all the rooms, calling our names, her face screwed up with the abnormality of it.

Buying the presents was a difficult business. Neddy was easy enough; you felt that anything at all would delight him, but Pearly was another matter altogether. There were so many things that didn't agree with her: chocolates gave her headaches, and so did anything with perfume in it; she didn't wear scarves or jewelry, and she thought that buying books was a waste of money when you could borrow them from the library for free. We walked around and around boutiques and gift shops and even Slasher's Discount Store, picking things up and examining them hopefully and then putting them back again when we thought of Pearly. Mrs. Capsella became slightly hysterical when I suggested she put back a giant box of toffees, reminding her that Pearly's teeth didn't seem quite real. She stalked out of Slasher's and collapsed tearfully on the nearest bus-stop seat.

I was a trifle concerned about Mrs. Capsella; she seemed rather lifeless, a shade of her former self. Living at the Blounts, keeping regular hours and having nothing much to do all day except read the kind of books she wrote herself, had worn her out. I knew she could hardly wait to get back to her scruffy house and clothes and husband. I felt that way myself; I longed to see a living room scattered all over with discarded clothes and newspapers and coffee cups.

She had now closed her eyes.

"What are you going to do about the present?" I urged.

She opened her eyes and said that Pearly Blount was a menace, and as soon as she'd got her strength, back she was going straight to the Misses Parrs' Haberdasher to buy a pair of Patons Beehive knitting needles.

"That will look pretty cheap," I said.

"Too bad," muttered Mrs. Capsella childishly.

"I know just the thing," I said.

"What?"

I wouldn't tell. I was so full of my idea that I didn't want to hear all the reasons why it mightn't be a good one. Mrs. Capsella limply handed over her wallet, and I ran all the way to the pet shop.

It wasn't at all the kind of dog I would have chosen for myself. I like big dogs, German shepherds or Irish setters, dogs with long tails and sturdy legs and deep, loud barks: This one was tiny, scarcely bigger than a kitten. It had long, fluffy, girly white hair and bright little blue eyes, but I knew it was just right for Pearly Blount. It went with her hair—it belonged, the fluffiness and the glittery eyes and the bright-pink tongue, the same shade as her fluffy woollies.

And I was right: Pearly loved it; she even brought it out to the front gate, cradled against her chest, to see us off in the taxi. It yapped in a shrill, ear-splitting fashion, but she didn't seem to notice. As the taxi driver started up his engine, Neddy put his head through the window. "You know," he said seriously, "dogs should rule the world."

"What?"

"Just what I said. Dogs should rule the world. When do you see dogs cheating on their Social Security, or dressing up in jeans and marching in demonstrations? When did you last see a dog with one of those punk hairdos, or a dog that voted Red?"

I was terribly glad to be going. "Right," I said faintly, treacherously.

"Okey-doke." He waved; so did Pearly. The taxi slid away. Mrs. Capsella and I fell back against the seats and slouched restfully. You couldn't do that in the Blounts' house; Pearly told you to sit up straight or you'd end up in a spinal brace.

As we turned the corner, the taxi driver asked Mrs. Capsella if the old guy had all his marbles.

"I'll have you know," Mrs. Capsella replied, "that my father is a perfectly normal man."

"He has a heart of gold," I added.

"Sorry, folks," said the taxi driver.

"I'll never use that word again," I sighed.

"What word?"

"Normal," I replied.